Fire danced through his veins.

Mary's lips were soft and warm, and they only increased Tony's appetite for more. Her breasts pushed against his chest and the heady scent of her surrounded him. The kiss went on for several long moments, and then she broke it and stepped back from him.

The flames of his own desire shot out of her eyes, letting him know that she'd been as moved by the kiss as he had. "That wasn't really a good idea," she said, her voice slightly husky.

He grinned at her. "It wasn't really a bad idea." He reached out and tucked a strand of her long hair behind her ear, his fingers noting the silky softness.

"Tony, it wouldn't be wise for us to indulge in any kind of a relationship other than what we have right now." She took a step back from him.

"Do we always have to be wise?" he countered.

"I try to be," she replied. Joey cried out from behind them. "Good night, Tony."

**Be sure to check out the next books
in this exciting miniseries:**

**Cowboys of Holiday Ranch—Where sun,
earth and hard work turn men into rugged
cowboys...and irresistible heroes!**

* * *

**If you're on Twitter, tell us what you
think of Harlequin Romantic Suspense!
#harlequinromsuspense**

Dear Reader,

Like my hero, Tony Nakni, I love autumn. I enjoy the cool evening breezes, the changing colors of the tree leaves and that crisp, clean scent that lingers in the air.

However, for Tony autumn brings big changes when his ex-girlfriend drops off a baby and tells him the child is his. Before he can ask any questions she's gone, and the cowboy is left with the three-month-old baby. In desperation he seeks the help of Mary Redwing, a woman who has secrets of her own.

Tony and Mary not only face an unexpected danger but also a surprising passion. In order to protect the child, they will not only have to put their lives on the line, but also their hearts.

Oh, yes, I love autumn, especially when it brings a shout of danger and a whisper of desire.

I hope you enjoy reading *Operation Cowboy Daddy*, the newest book in the Cowboys of Holiday Ranch series.

Happy reading!

Carla Cassidy

OPERATION COWBOY DADDY

Carla Cassidy

HARLEQUIN® ROMANTIC SUSPENSE

Recycling programs
for this product may
not exist in your area.

ISBN-13: 978-0-373-28197-8

Operation Cowboy Daddy

Copyright © 2016 by Carla Bracale

HARLEQUIN®
www.Harlequin.com

Printed in U.S.A.

Carla Cassidy is an award-winning, *New York Times* bestselling author who has written more than one hundred and twenty novels for Harlequin. In 1995, she won Best Silhouette Romance from *RT Book Reviews* for *Anything for Danny*. In 1998, she won a Career Achievement Award for Best Innovative Series from *RT Book Reviews*. Carla believes the only thing better than curling up with a good book to read is sitting down at the computer with a good story to write.

Books by Carla Cassidy

Harlequin Romantic Suspense

Cowboys of Holiday Ranch

A Real Cowboy
Cowboy of Interest
Cowboy Under Fire
Cowboy At Arms
Operation Cowboy Daddy

The Coltons of Texas

Colton Cowboy Hideout

The Coltons of Oklahoma

The Colton Bodyguard

Men of Wolf Creek

Cold Case, Hot Accomplice
Lethal Lawman
Lone Wolf Standing

Chapter 1

This was Tony Nakni's favorite time, when the day slowly faded and took on the slightly purple shades of dusk as the sun sank behind the horizon.

He sat outside, in front of his bunk-room door, and drew in a deep breath of the early September evening air. Cicadas clicked and whirred their songs from nearby trees and a cow lowed from the pasture in the distance.

The twelve-unit bunkhouse was quiet for now, but Tony knew it was the calm before a brief storm. In the next half hour or so most of the other cowboys would explode out of their rooms, all of them cleaned up and ready for a Saturday night out on the town.

They'd all head to the Watering Hole. The bar was the place to go for drinking, playing pool or dancing in the small town of Bitterroot, Oklahoma.

Tony only rarely joined the other men on their weekly foray of cutting loose after a long week of work on the ranch. He preferred to unwind by watching the sunset, having a beer and, until recently, talking to Dusty Crawford, who had lived in the bunk room next to Tony's.

But two weeks ago, Dusty had moved from the Holiday ranch into a house in town with Trisha Cahill and her three-year-old son, Cooper. Dusty had chosen a life path that Tony had no interest in following. Tony had been alone for as long as he could remember and he was most comfortable that way.

He reached down and grabbed a beer from the small cooler at his feet. He twisted off the top, tossed the lid into the cooler, took a sip and leaned back in his chair.

In the distance, lights began to glow from the windows of the big house where Cassie Peterson lived. It was hard to believe that it had been almost five months since owner Cass Holiday had been killed in a spring tornado that had ripped through the area. Everyone had been surprised to learn that she'd left the ranch to her niece, Cassie. Cassie was New York City born and raised and since she'd taken over the ranch there had been many adjustments.

The sixty-eight-year-old Cass had been the only person Tony had completely trusted on the face of the earth. All of the cowboys on the ranch had been a bit lost since her death.

He shoved thoughts of Cass out of his head and instead focused his attention on the colorful sunset currently taking place in the western sky. As far as he was concerned, Bitterroot, Oklahoma, was a little piece of heaven on earth.

He turned his attention to the right as he heard a door open and then smelled the scent of minty soap and heavy spicy cologne.

"Hey, brother." Sawyer Quincy greeted Tony with a grin. "Why don't you splash on some good-smelling stuff and come with us into town. Maybe you can find yourself a sexy female to warm your cold, lonely bed."

Tony grinned back at the tall, russet-haired cowboy. "You have enough smelly stuff on for the both of us. Besides, you never come home with a female. You're usually carried back from town by the other men."

Sawyer's inability to hold his liquor was legendary. It took only a couple of beers for him to be half-comatose. "Don't remind me," he said ruefully. "It's embarrassing that I can ride a wild bronco and wrestle a steer to the ground in record time, but I can't drink more than three or four beers without getting totally plastered."

"Have you ever considered not drinking beer at all?"

Sawyer looked at him in mock horror. "What kind of a cowboy doesn't drink beer?"

Before Tony could reply, several other ranch hands made an appearance from around the corner of the building. Adam Benson, the ranch foreman, was followed by Mac McBride, Brody Booth and Clay Madison.

"You keeping the home fires burning again tonight, Tony?" Adam asked.

"Yeah, I'm looking forward to nothing more exciting than a good night's sleep," he replied.

"I'll kiss a beautiful lady for you," Clay said with his usual bravado. "Heck, maybe I'll kiss two."

Tony laughed. "Clay, if you actually did as much as you talked, you'd be a real legend. As it is, you're only a legend in your own mind," Tony teased.

The others hooted with laughter. There was a bit more ribbing of each other and then they all headed to the outbuilding, where the vehicles were parked. Minutes later headlights wove through the semidarkness in the direction toward town.

Tony finished his beer and grabbed a second one. Tomorrow was Sunday and in the rotation of the ranch work, it was a day he was off duty.

He had no real plans for the next day. He might go into town and see about getting a new pair of boots, or he might not. He tried to live in the moment, never looking to the future or dwelling on the past.

By the time he finished his second beer the dark of night had settled in. He grabbed his cooler and folding chair and carried them into his room.

All of the living quarters for the cowboys who worked the Holiday ranch were the same. A twin bed was on one side of the room and a chest of drawers was on the other. There was also a small closet and a bathroom with a shower.

Most of the men who lived here had added personal touches to make the rooms their own over the years. But other than the brown cowboy hat and gun and holster on top of the dresser, and the clothes in the closet, Tony's room was exactly the same as it had been when he'd been a fifteen-year-old runaway and Cass Holiday had taken a chance on him.

If she hadn't hired him on here, there was no question in his mind that he would have more than likely died on the streets of Oklahoma City. He probably would have been beaten to death—not for who he was or any action he'd taken, but rather for what he was.

He pulled out the strip of rawhide that he used to tie back his black hair during the day and then stripped down to his boxers and got into bed.

The only time any ghosts from the past ever threatened him was in the quiet minutes just before he fell asleep, in the darkened privacy of his room.

Half-breed. Your mother didn't want you and your father was a drunk who was gone long before you were born. You don't belong anywhere. You have no place in this world. You're just lucky we took you in.

He consciously shoved the hurtful words away. He wasn't a little boy anymore, wondering why his foster parents treated him so differently from their own children.

He fell asleep with the ghosts from his youth silenced. He wasn't sure how long he'd been asleep when rapid knocking sounded at his door.

A glance at the clock let him know it was almost one. He muttered a small curse and got out of bed, fully expecting one of his fellow cowboys who wanted to share the drunken escapades of the evening with him.

He pulled open the door and stared in stunned surprise at the blond-haired, blue-eyed woman who stood before him. "Amy…what are you doing here?"

It had been a little over a year ago since Tony had last seen Amy Kincaid. He'd been just a bit crazy over her, until he realized she was more than just a little bit crazy herself. She was achingly thin and sported a yellowing bruise on the side of her face.

"Tony, I'm in trouble." She cast a glance over her skinny shoulder and then looked at him again, her eyes huge and simmering with what appeared to be barely suppressed terror.

She'd pulled her car up just outside the bunkhouse, had driven across the lawn from where the driveway ended in the distance. The engine was still running.

"Amy, what's going on? Come inside and talk to me," he replied.

She shook her head. "I've got to go, but I need you to step up."

Tony frowned. "Step up?"

She turned and ran to her car and opened the back door. She pulled out a medium-sized suitcase and then a car seat with a sleeping baby inside.

When she returned to his door, Tony stared at her in bewilderment. "Would you tell me what's going on?"

"This is your son. His name is Joey." Tears welled up in her eyes. "I can't take care of him right now." Once again she shot a frantic look over her shoulder. "I've got to go, Tony." She grabbed his forearm, her fingers feverish and her sharp nails biting into his skin. "Please… protect him from evil." She turned and ran for her car.

"Amy, wait!" Tony shouted after her, but she didn't stop, didn't even hesitate. She jumped into the driver seat and then tore off toward the ranch exit.

Two other doors flew open. Clay came out of one and Sawyer stumbled out of the other one. "Whaz goin' on?" Sawyer mumbled with a slight slur. "Hey, what's that doing here?" he asked as he stared down at the sleeping little boy.

"It's not a 'that,' it's a boy," Tony replied absently. He was still trying to process what had just happened. *This is your son. Protect him from evil.* "Amy just dropped him off. She said he's my son and it was time for me to step up."

"Congrats, man," Sawyer said. "I'll get you a cigar with a bright blue band around it tomorrow." He turned and went back into his room.

"Amy? Wow, did you know she was pregnant when the two of you stopped seeing each other?" Clay asked.

"No, I didn't have a clue. I haven't seen or heard from her in a year. She moved to Oklahoma City while we were dating…" Tony broke off and continued to stare down at the little boy with his shock of black hair and chubby cheeks.

"Are you sure he's really yours?" Clay asked.

Tony gazed at his blond-haired fellow cowboy. "At this moment I'm not sure of anything."

"What are you going to do?"

"Right now I guess I'm going to get him out of the chilly night air and then I'll see what tomorrow brings." Tony bent down and picked up the car seat while Clay grabbed the suitcase and together they went into Tony's room.

Tony set the baby seat on the bed and Clay placed

the suitcase on the floor. "Are you going to be all right with this for now?" Clay asked.

"I suppose I have to be," Tony replied, his heart beating an unsteady rhythm. Heck, he had no idea if he was going to be all right. He didn't know anything about babies.

"Let me know if you need anything." Clay left the room and closed the door behind him.

Tony remained standing next to his bed and stared at the sleeping child. Tony had never wanted to be a husband and he'd certainly never wanted to be a father and Amy had known that when they'd dated. He'd made that very clear to her.

She'd looked so terrified. What was going on in her life that had prompted her to drop off her child with a man she hadn't seen in over a year? Was he really Tony's son? And why had she said to protect him from evil?

At that moment the little boy's eyes fluttered open. His features screwed up and he began to cry.

He had to find the bitch.

Ash Moreland tightened his grip on his steering wheel as he turned down another Oklahoma City street, seeking Amy's car. He had to find her and make sure she didn't talk, that she didn't tell anyone what she had seen.

If she'd just stayed in the bedroom like he'd told her to, then she wouldn't have seen him slit Barker's throat. After that, she'd gone to the bedroom and throughout the rest of the evening she'd acted like everything was okay. But Ash had known she was shaken up and sure enough at just after midnight she'd crept out of bed.

He'd stayed in bed and listened to her as she'd gone into the baby's room, and minutes later he'd heard the closing of the front door. He could have stopped her at any moment, but he was curious. In all honesty he'd been amused by her pathetic move to leave him.

He'd followed her the almost sixty miles to Bitterroot and had watched her hand his baby over to another man. That, in and of itself, was an unforgivable betrayal.

She'd left Bitterroot and then driven back to Oklahoma City. He'd been tracking her for the past couple of hours, wondering what she was going to do, where she might go. If she'd gone anywhere near a police station, she would have never made it inside alive.

She had no friends and she had no money. Ash had seen to that during the last year that the two of them had been together. She belonged to him, just like the lucrative drug business he ran and just like the house where they lived, which was filled with fine and expensive items. Amy was his possession and Ash would decide when it was time to get rid of a possession.

He'd had her car taillights in his sights until about fifteen minutes ago, when she'd managed to give him the slip. He drove the dark streets slowly, his initial amusement long gone and rage rising with each moment that passed.

If he didn't find her tonight, then he'd assign half a dozen of his men to hunt her down. Sooner or later she was going to run out of gas and out of options.

Sooner or later she'd probably come crawling back

to him, begging him to forgive her for running away, sniveling to him for a fix that would make her well.

He'd hunt her down tonight and then tomorrow he'd go get his baby, the son who was his flesh, his blood, and who would one day take over Ash's kingdom.

It was the longest night Tony had ever known and in his past he'd had many long nights. It wasn't the company of Joey in his room that kept him from sleep, although certainly the tiny boy made his presence known several times.

The suitcase was filled with bottles and formula, disposable diapers and clothes. Twice in the night Tony had given Joey bottles and changed diapers, thankful that the baby had then seemed perfectly satisfied and had fallen back asleep.

Unfortunately sleep hadn't come to Tony. He'd lain in bed with Joey between him and the wall and listened to the little boy breathe as thoughts had whirled in his head.

Was the boy really his? He supposed it was possible. He and Amy had certainly enjoyed an intense physical relationship, but she had assured him she was on birth control and he'd taken extra protection.

He didn't even know how old the baby was, or if Amy had been seeing Tony exclusively at the time they'd been dating each other. When he'd broken things off with her, he'd certainly suspected there was somebody else in her life.

Why hadn't she told him she was pregnant? If the little boy was his, then why hadn't she come to him and told him? She knew where he lived. She knew where he worked. Where had she been for the last year and what had she been doing?

And what was Tony going to do until Amy returned? He wasn't cut out for being a father. He didn't know anything about babies other than they were hungry little pooping beasts. Hopefully, she intended to show up here before another night fell.

Those were only a few of the questions that kept him staring at the ceiling until dawn broke and Joey awakened. He gave him a bottle, changed his diaper and clothes and then placed him in his car seat to travel to the cowboy dining room, where Tony could grab some breakfast and figure out what in the heck he was going to do with Joey until Amy returned.

At least he'd managed to make it through the night and the baby didn't seem any worse for it, he thought as he circled around the row of rooms to the large dining and rec room in the back of the building.

Sawyer was the first person who saw him walk in. The lanky cowboy's brown eyes widened. "Jeez, Tony, I thought I had a beer-induced delusion last night, but it was real. You really have a kid."

"I have possession of one, but I'm not sure he's really mine," Tony replied.

The other men in the dining room gathered around and once again Tony told everyone about Amy's unexpected middle-of-the-night stork delivery.

"How are you going to work and take care of a baby?" Brody Booth asked.

"And what in the heck do you know about taking

care of a baby?" Jerod Steen stared at Joey as if he was a species of animal the dark-haired, dark-eyed man had never seen before.

"What are you going to do if Amy never comes back?" Flint McCay asked.

All of the worries that had kept Tony up all night crashed into him again. What on earth was he going to do? "I don't have answers to any of those questions. I've just got to have some time to figure things out."

Mac McBride leaned down and grinned at Joey. "Aren't you the cutest little buckaroo we've ever had in this dining room?" he said in the musical voice that, along with his guitar, often entertained the men in the evenings.

Little Joey, who had remained silent and somber until that moment, suddenly laughed. The infectious giggling filled up the entire room and all of the men stared at him in awe.

Tony steeled his heart. There was no way he was going to get attached to Joey. He refused to be moved by Joey's smiles and antics. All he had to do was figure out exactly what he was going to do with the baby until Amy returned.

"Big changes coming," Halena announced.

Mary Redwing turned around from the scrambled eggs she'd been preparing to eye her grandmother curiously. "And you know this how?"

"I dream-walked last night in my sleep." Bright morning sunshine poured in through the windows to sparkle on Halena Redwing's long, thick silver braids.

She was clad in a pair of red-and-black polka-dotted sleep pants and a ruffled bright pink blouse.

"And where did you go?" Mary's heart filled with love as she gazed at the woman who had raised her, a woman who at eighty-six years old now shared Mary's home. Halena had always been eccentric but had grown even more so with each year that passed.

"I went to Kansas."

"Oh." Mary blinked in surprise. Normally Halena dream-walked to strange and foreign places she didn't recognize. "Hang on and you can tell me more."

She turned back to the eggs and scooped a portion out on each plate that waited with bacon and toast already on them. She carried the plates across the room and joined her grandmother at the table.

"Okay, now, what did you find in Kansas?" Mary asked.

"A tornado and a tin man."

Mary thought back over the past week and tried to remember what movies her grandmother might have watched. A month ago she'd gotten up early one morning and had announced that robots would soon be taking over the world. That had occurred after the previous night's *Terminator* marathon.

"So you dream-walked in a terrible storm and met a heartless man," Mary replied.

Halena nodded. "The tornado is a portent of great change coming and we have to beware of the tin man who comes. Now, let's eat."

Mary picked up a piece of bacon and chewed thoughtfully. She didn't have to beware of any man. Her future had no place for a man and at thirty-two years old she'd come to terms with the fact that she would live her life alone, without a husband…without a family.

She was fulfilled by her work, by the friendships she shared and with the often amusing and always wise company of her grandmother. That was enough for her. It had to be enough.

"What's on your agenda for today?" Mary asked after they'd eaten and as they cleaned up the breakfast dishes.

"I'm going to try to finish up that turquoise skirt so I can get started on another one. I'd like to sew at least ten more before the craft show," Halena replied.

Despite her advancing age, Halena still made beautiful skirts with beaded detail that was stunning, along with the more traditional Choctaw dresses. They always sold well at the annual Oklahoma Days Craft Fair.

"Ten skirts in two weeks, that's a pretty tall order," Mary replied.

"The more skirts, the more new movies I can buy," Halena replied.

A year ago, when Halena had been recovering from a mild heart attack, a friend had given her a DVD player and a handful of movies. Since that time she was movie-obsessed.

"And I'm going to work on some baskets out on the back porch. It's going to be such a beautiful day," Mary replied.

Halena nodded. "It's always good to have a plan. And now I think it's time to get to work. I need to get these skirts done as quickly as possible."

As Halena headed to her bedroom, Mary smiled in amusement. Her grandmother was an amusing blend of old tradition and new-world savvy. She was often a guest speaker at the Durant Indian Nation grade school, where she spoke about the history and culture of their people, and she also had a blog with tons of followers, where she talked about everything from how to properly fold a bath towel to sex and love tips.

The screened-in back porch was Mary's work space as long as the weather allowed. When it got colder or was too rainy, she moved inside to the spare bedroom, but today was positively gorgeous.

She stepped outside to the musical sound of wind chimes dancing in the light breeze. The scent of autumn was in the air and the river cane she used to make the baskets she sold tickled her nose.

She'd built a successful business for herself, selling baskets and pottery and other items not only at craft fairs, but also through her internet site.

As she sat at the long worktable, it didn't take her long to lose herself in the artistry of weaving. She worked here most mornings and then after lunch her grandmother often joined her. The two would work and chat until dinnertime and then move back inside for the evening. After supper, Halena worked on her blog or watched movies, while Mary checked in with the two people who helped her with her web-based business.

"It's going to be a long winter," Halena said as she settled into the cushy porch chair after lunch. The skirt she was hand-sewing was a beautiful spill of turquoise in her lap.

"And how do you know that?" Mary asked.

"The leaves in the trees have whispered to me that the snow will come early and stay late," she said.

"Last year didn't the leaves in the trees whisper to you that we'd have an unusually wet summer?" Mary asked in amusement. It had been the driest summer on record.

Halena smiled with a glint in her eyes. "Okay, I'll admit that sometimes the leaves lie to me."

Mary laughed, but her laughter was cut short by a loud knock on the front door. "I wonder who that could be," she said. She got up from the table and hurried through the house to answer.

She opened the door and stared at the man on her porch in stunned surprise. "Tony," she said in shock. The last time she'd seen the handsome cowboy had been a little over a year ago, when he and her friend Amy had come to visit several times.

He held on to a baby car seat with a bright-eyed, chubby-cheeked infant tucked beneath a blue blanket. Tony was not only clad in jeans, a white T-shirt and a brown cowboy hat, but he also wore an air of utter desperation.

"Mary, can I come in?" he asked.

"Of course." She stepped aside and as he swept past her to enter the living room, he smelled of not only sunshine and fresh air, but also a woodsy cologne that was instantly appealing.

She hated the way her heart beat just a little faster at the mere sight of him. The very first time she'd met him her heart had reacted the same way, and it had shamed her, since he was her friend's boyfriend.

She closed the door behind him and motioned him to sit on the sofa. What was he doing here? And why did he have a baby, who cooed softly as he set the carrier on the floor next to him?

"Have you been in touch with Amy lately?" he asked as she sat in the chair opposite the sofa. He took off his hat and placed it next to him.

"No. The last time I spoke to her was about six months ago. Why?"

"She came by the ranch last night and said she was in trouble." He glanced down at the baby and his jaw tightened. "She told me the baby is mine and his name is Joey, then she jumped into her car and drove off. I need to find her."

Oh, Amy, what kind of trouble have you found this time? "I'm sorry, Tony, I don't know what to tell you. The last time I talked to her she was living in Oklahoma City with a man she met not long after the two of you went your separate ways. I tried to call her a while ago, but the phone number I had for her was no good."

Tony's eyes bored into hers with intensity. A woman could fall into those dark depths. "Do you remember the name of the man?"

Mary frowned thoughtfully and tried to remember the last conversation she'd had with her friend. "No, I don't think she mentioned his name to me."

Her gaze drifted down to the baby. He smiled and cooed to her and a wave of unexpected anguish swept through her, an anguish she'd believed she'd made peace with a long time ago.

"Did you know she was pregnant?" Tony asked.

Mary nodded. "She told me she was pregnant with your child when she first took a test."

Tony's strong features expressed bewilderment. "Why didn't she tell me? Why didn't she come to me?"

"I don't know, Tony. I certainly encouraged her to do so at the time." But there was no telling Amy anything when she didn't want to listen. "Besides, she made me promise I wouldn't tell you."

He leaned back against the beige sofa, his disturbed energy filling the air. "Do you know for sure that he's mine?"

Mary's heart squeezed tight as she thought about her troubled friend. "I can only go by what she told me at the time, but I know when she did tell me she was already living with the other man." She knew that Tony probably understood as well as she did that Amy wasn't always a reliable source of truthfulness.

He remained silent for several long minutes, his gaze directed someplace over her shoulder. Tony Nakni obviously had Native American blood. His skin tone was a warm bronze and his straight black hair was a thing of glory, falling to the middle of his shoulders.

And those broad shoulders accentuated his slim hips and long legs. Physically he stirred something in Mary that had been dormant for a very long time.

His gaze returned to her and he leaned forward. "I need your help, Mary."

At that moment Halena came in from the back porch

and stood in the doorway between the living room and the kitchen. "Grandmother, do you remember Tony Nakni? He came to visit a couple of times with Amy."

"I don't remember what we had for breakfast this morning," Halena replied as she eyed Tony with a touch of suspicion. "Is that your baby?"

Tony hesitated a moment. "I don't know," he finally replied. "What I do know for sure is that I need help." He looked back at Mary.

"What kind of help?" she asked.

"I'll pay you whatever it takes if you'll take care of Joey just until I can find Amy," he said. She stared at him in stunned surprise and he quickly continued, "I know you're a good woman, Mary. I wouldn't trust him with anyone else, but I have to work during the day and I don't live in a place that would be healthy for a baby. Besides, I don't know what I'm doing. I know I'm asking a lot, but I don't have anyplace else to turn. It should only be for a couple of days or so."

Mary was speechless. In a million years she wouldn't have been able to anticipate a visit from Tony, let alone the favor that he asked of her. He had also just spoken more words than he had during all the visits when he and Amy had been here before.

She didn't want to get involved with this. Anything that had to do with Amy always wound up to be a big mess. Besides, he was talking about her taking on a huge responsibility.

Still, as Joey cooed and waved his hands in the air as if catching imaginary butterflies, myriad emotions surged up inside her.

"Okay, I'll do it," she heard herself say.

Tony jumped up off the sofa. "Thank you so much," he said fervently. He picked up his hat. "I'll just head into town and get some things for you that you'll need."

"Don't thank me yet, you haven't heard my terms," Mary replied. If the baby was Tony's, then he wasn't going to get off so easily. She wasn't just going to take care of little Joey without him being a part of it.

"Terms?" He looked at her warily.

"Joey can stay here with us, but when you get off work in the evenings, you need to be here with him." All she was thinking of was what was best for the child. It had nothing to do with the fact that she was intensely attracted to Tony.

"That's not a problem," he replied. The darkness that had filled his eyes dissipated somewhat for the first time since he'd walked through the door. "I can't tell you how much I appreciate this."

He began to inch toward the front door. "I've got a suitcase full of stuff that Amy left with him. I'll go get that now and then I'll pick up some more things in town and be back here later this afternoon."

"I'll walk out with you for the suitcase," Mary replied.

They left the house and headed toward his black king-cab pickup parked in her driveway. "It's possible Amy will show up in the next day or so," he said. He pulled the suitcase out of the pickup bed and then frowned. "She didn't look good, Mary. I think she's back on drugs."

Mary's heart sank, although she wasn't surprised. Amy had fought addiction issues for years. "Let's just hope whatever is going on with her life, she gets it together soon and comes back for her son."

"This arrangement isn't going to cause issues with your boyfriend or a significant other, is it?" he asked worriedly.

"Since I don't have a significant other or a boyfriend, there's no problem," she replied.

Moments later she watched as Tony's truck disappeared in the distance. She gripped the suitcase handle tightly and wondered what she had just gotten herself into.

She should have never agreed to this. The last thing she needed was to have a baby in the house to remind her of all her inadequacies. But Tony had looked so desperate.

It's going to be just fine, she assured herself. It was possible Amy had already returned to the Holiday ranch looking for Tony and her baby.

With this positive thought in mind she headed inside. Halena remained standing in the same place she'd been during the conversation with Tony, only now she had deep lines etched across her forehead.

"Big changes," she said. "And a tin man… You'd better guard yourself, my Mary. The leaves are whispering to me that this is not a good thing."

Mary released an uneasy laugh. "But, Grandmother, sometimes the leaves lie to you."

Halena's eyes remained dark and troubled. "And sometimes they don't," she replied.

Chapter 2

Tony had forgotten about Mary Redwing's beauty. Of course, the last time he'd seen her he'd been completely besotted by Amy's curly blond hair, bright blue eyes and infectious giggles.

He'd been relieved when he'd thought about Mary that morning. She was not only an old friend to Amy, but also a woman who had given him the impression of great stability and strength on the few times he'd seen her.

Still, he'd never really noticed the richness of her long black hair in the single braid down her back, or her beautiful doe eyes, or her full lips and high cheekbones.

She'd been clad in a pair of tight jeans that showcased her long legs and her brown T-shirt had fit perfectly across her breasts and slender waist.

He was just so glad she'd agreed to take care of the boy. Before he'd thought about Mary, Tony had spent the morning not just worried about what he was going to do, but concerned that he might do something wrong, or not do something at all that Joey needed.

The first thing he intended to do before he did any shopping was get a quick bite to eat at the Bitterroot Café. His nerves had been so shot that morning he'd barely eaten any breakfast and lunchtime had already come and gone.

His stomach gurgled in anticipation as he pulled into the café parking lot. He frowned when he saw two familiar pickups also there. The men from the Humes ranch must be having a late lunch, too.

As far as all the cowboys on the Holiday ranch were concerned, all the men who worked on the neighboring ranch were lowlifes and creeps. One of them was now in jail, looking at plenty of prison time for kidnapping Trisha Cahill, who worked here as a waitress and who was the love of Dusty's life.

Tony got out of his truck and walked through the café door. He immediately spied Lloyd Green, Zeke Osmond and Ace Sanders from the Humes place seated in a booth. He headed for an empty stool at the long counter, pleased to see Trisha working that area.

She greeted him with a huge smile. "A little late for you today, Tony," she said.

"I had a few other things to attend to this morning."

"Clay and Sawyer were in a little while ago and filled me in on the latest news. Where is the baby now?"

"Do you know Mary Redwing?" he asked.

Trisha nodded. "A nice woman. Her grandmother is definitely a pip."

"They're going to take care of the baby until Amy shows back up again…hopefully in the next day or two. How are you and Dusty doing? I haven't had much of a chance to talk to him the last couple of days. You still like living with that crazy cowboy?"

She flashed him a bright smile again. "He's wonderful, we're wonderful."

"When are the wedding bells going to ring?"

"We're not having a real wedding. We're just going to sneak away one of these weekends and get married at city hall. We're already married in our hearts."

"He's a lucky man, Trisha."

"And I'm a lucky woman. And now, what can I get for you?"

He ordered a hamburger and fries and ate quickly as he mentally tried to make a list of what Mary might need.

He was almost finished eating when the men from the Humes ranch walked over to him. "Hey, Tony, I heard through the grapevine that you have a little papoose," Lloyd Green said and then snickered.

"Are you going to teach him how to hunt with arrows?" Zeke asked.

"Or maybe how to scalp somebody?" Ace added.

Tony turned around on the stool to face the men, his blood boiling at their utter disrespect, the vile offensiveness of their words.

Flashbacks from his painful childhood raced through

his head, flashbacks that had made Tony hate the very blood that flowed through his veins.

All three men balled their hands into fists. It was obvious they were spoiling for a little entertainment in the form of a fight. Tension snapped in the air.

"Ignore them, Tony," Trisha said softly, yet urgently.

He had been taught by the tough Cass Holiday to never start a fight, but she'd also told him never to walk away from one.

He was just about to get off his stool when the chief of police, Dillon Bowie, entered the café. "Afternoon, gentlemen." His gray eyes narrowed. "Is there a problem here?"

"No problem." Lloyd moved the toothpick in his mouth from one side to the other as he backed away from Tony's stool. The two younger men followed his example and stepped back.

"We were just on our way out," Zeke mumbled. The three hurried out the door.

"They're a bunch of jerks," Trisha exclaimed as Dillon took the stool next to Tony's.

The lawman's eyes bore into Tony's. "Don't tell me there's new bad blood brewing between all of you."

"Like Trisha said, they're just a bunch of jerks," Tony replied as his blood slowly returned to a more normal temperature. "Anything new on the investigation?"

Tony didn't have to say specifically what investigation—there was only one that he was interested in and only one that had been the talk of the town for months.

Dillon's eyes darkened. "Nothing new."

"Would you tell me if there was something new?" Tony asked.

Dillon gave him a dry grin. "Probably not."

Tony knew that he and every other cowboy on the ranch were suspects in the fifteen-year-old murder case that had rocked not only the people on the Holiday ranch, but also the entire town of Bitterroot.

"I've got to get moving," Tony said as he stood. "I've got things to attend to."

"I'm sure I'll see you later," Dillon said.

"'Bye, Tony," Trisha added.

Once he was back in his truck, thoughts of the murders filled Tony's mind. It had been just after Cass's death in the aftermath of the spring tornado that the skeletons of seven young men had been found buried under an old building that was being torn down.

The murders had been committed around the time period that Cass had brought in twelve teenagers who had been living on the streets in Oklahoma City to work on her ranch, making all of the men still working there today potential suspects.

He shoved these thoughts aside as he pulled into the parking lot of the Bitterroot General Store. Inside, a person could buy everything from a fancy evening dress to a part for a lawn mower. He hoped he could find anything that Mary might need to take care of the baby.

An hour later he finished placing the last item in the bed of his pickup and then headed back to Mary's house. He knew this was only a temporary arrangement. He had to find Amy. He had to know if the baby was really his, or if she'd lied about who the baby's daddy was to Mary.

One of the reasons he'd stopped seeing Amy was because of her lies. He frowned and tightened his grip on the steering wheel. What kind of trouble was she in and when would she reappear?

He couldn't believe it had taken him so long to think of Amy's friend, but the shock of being left with a baby had numbed his brain.

It was almost four when he pulled back into Mary's driveway and sat for a moment as he gazed at the house before him. The ranch-style home was on a huge lot with tall cottonwood trees along the back perimeter.

It exuded a sense of welcoming, with its warm dark beige color and the last of the summer flowers spilling a colorful display into flower beds across the front of the house and in pots on the front porch.

A sense of fear whipped through him. What if in the hours he'd been gone Mary had changed her mind? He meant nothing to Mary Redwing and she certainly had no reason to take on his troubles.

If truth be told, he knew very little about her. He knew only that she'd been a kind and caring friend to Amy and that her reputation around town was stellar.

He got out of his truck and grabbed several of the bags, filled with formula and diapers, and then knocked on the front door.

Mary opened the door to allow him inside. The air smelled of something cooking and Joey was asleep on a blanket in the middle of the living room. There was no sign of Mary's grandmother.

Mary gestured for him to follow her into the kitchen, where he placed the plastic bags on the top of the table. "There's more in the truck," he said.

She frowned at him. "You said this was just for a couple of days."

"It is," he assured her. Stress welled up inside him. What if Amy didn't make contact within the next day or two? Then what was he going to do?

He shoved these thoughts aside. He couldn't think about that scenario right now. "I bought a small playpen for him to sleep in and a bouncy chair thingy that Jenna McCain in the general store insisted I needed. I'll just go grab them and be right back."

Once again Mary met him at the door and this time indicated he follow her down a hallway and into what appeared to be a storage room. Plastic shelving rose from floor to ceiling along one side of the room, each shelf holding colorful multishaped baskets, beautiful pottery items and a variety of clothing carefully folded.

"You can set up the playpen in here." She pointed to an empty space near the window. "I need to get back to the kitchen. You can come back in there when you're finished in here."

Tony watched as she left the room and disappeared down the hallway. He set the playpen box down on the carpeting and opened it.

He was just placing the pads around the sides when he sensed somebody nearby. He turned to see Halena standing in the doorway. "Hello again," he said.

"Tony Nakni. Are you a good Choctaw warrior?" Her gaze was dark and unfathomable.

He didn't know how to answer. He wasn't a good Choctaw anything. He knew nothing about that part of his DNA. He'd been taught from a young age that his Native American blood was something to be ashamed of.

Still, he had a feeling that the question was far more important than anything Mary had asked him and that his answer might screw up this whole arrangement.

"I try to be," he finally replied.

Halena stared at him for another long minute. Her piercing gaze seemed to be probing into the very soul he believed he didn't possess and then she turned and walked away.

"I knew that girl was big trouble from the time she was young," Halena said as she came into the kitchen. "And I'm not sure that man in there is any better."

Mary turned from the stove, where she'd been stirring a big pot of stew. "None of that matters. What's important right now is the baby."

Halena sat at the table. "I know you, my granddaughter. I know your heart and I don't want you getting involved in somebody else's problems. Your spirit is very fragile and I don't want it to be further broken by anyone or anything."

"Don't worry about me," Mary assured her. "And my spirit is just fine." She opened the oven door and bent down to pull out a dish of thick corn bread.

Her grandmother was worried about the baby weaving a basket of love in her heart. But Mary wasn't going to allow that to happen. She would feed and change the little fellow for the few days he'd be here, but there was no way she intended to allow him into her heart. This was just a temporary situation and she couldn't allow herself to embrace Joey.

Still, the very heart she wanted to deny accelerated its beats as Tony walked into the kitchen. "The playpen is all set up with sheets and I put the bouncy thingy in the living room. I also bought a few little toys Jenna said would be age-appropriate. They're also in a bag in the living room."

"Thank you, it sounds like you got everything we might need," Mary replied. "We're just about to eat. You'll join us." She said it as a statement rather than a question. It was still early and as far as she was concerned he was officially on daddy duty for the rest of the evening.

"Uh…okay," he replied, appearing immensely uncomfortable. "Can I do anything to help?"

"Check on your son," Halena said as she rose from the table. "We'll take care of the meal."

It always made Mary nervous when her grandmother grew too quiet, and it was a silent Halena that helped her set the table and fill water glasses for the evening meal.

When the food was on the table, Mary went to the doorway that separated the kitchen from the living room. Tony sat on the edge of the sofa and stared at the sleeping baby. Bewilderment radiated from him, reminding her that he'd been thrust into this drama as unexpectedly as she had been.

"Tony," she said softly. "Dinner is ready."

He looked up at her and his eyes quickly shuttered.

He followed her into the kitchen and she motioned him into a chair. The pot of stew was the centerpiece and the slabs of corn bread were on the side, along with butter and honey.

"This all looks and smells delicious," he said.

"Mary knows her way around the kitchen," Halena replied. She pulled the stew closer to her and began to ladle it into her bowl. "And you, Tony Nakni…what do you know about life?"

He looked at her grandmother in surprise. She'd asked him a question he didn't seem to know how to answer.

"Grandmother, behave yourself," Mary said with a small laugh.

"I'm old enough that I don't have to behave myself anymore," Halena replied. "I've earned the right with age to do and say what I want. If I wish to dance naked in a rainstorm, I will. If I decide to wear a winter hat in July, it's okay. And that's that." She looked at Mary and then at Tony, as if daring either one of them to disagree with her.

"And that's that," Mary agreed with amusement.

Tony's eyes lightened and his lips twitched, as if he was controlling a smile. He filled his bowl and then slathered a piece of corn bread with butter.

It was the first hint of a smile she'd seen since he'd arrived here earlier in the day. She wasn't sure she wanted to see a real smile. She remembered when he'd come to visit with Amy those couple of times and how that expression had lit up his face and created a warmth in her…a warmth she had no right to feel. She still didn't have that right.

"Do you have any idea where Amy might be now?" she asked.

He shook his head. "I know she was living in Oklahoma City and I'm hoping she's still somewhere in that area," he replied. "She doesn't have any relatives that she ever mentioned. I know her parents are dead."

"They were both addicts," Mary replied. "When we were young, Amy spent most of her time at my parents' house. She was like an adopted daughter to my mother and father and then to my grandmother."

"She was broken as a child and she's still broken," Halena said. "Why would you choose to date a woman with such problems?"

Mary knew the answer. Amy was beautiful, and when she was clean and sober, she was effervescent and funny and loving. Any man would be drawn to her.

Tony set down his spoon and met Halena's gaze. "When I first started dating her, I had no clue about the demons she was fighting. I made it clear to her from the very beginning that I wasn't looking for marriage and I had no wish for children. She told me she was on the same page as me and we were both just enjoying each other's company. It was only as the relationship went on that alarm bells began to ring in my head." He frowned and looked beyond Halena's shoulder to the window, as if he was reluctant to say anything bad.

"She started lying to you," Mary said softly. "And she became unreliable. She didn't show up where she was supposed to, and when pressed about where she was, she became combative."

Tony looked at her in surprise. "Yes, exactly."

"I love Amy like a sister, but I know the pattern. I only hope she didn't use during her pregnancy," she replied.

Tony's eyes widened. "Do you think it's possible that she did? Maybe I should make an appointment for the baby to see a doctor to make sure everything is okay."

"That might not be a bad idea," Mary agreed, although during the hours she'd been with Joey she hadn't seen anything that concerned her.

"And while I'm at it, I'll have Dr. Rivers do a paternity test." Tony's cheeks flushed with faint color.

That might not be a bad idea, either, Mary thought, although she didn't say it aloud. Just because Amy had told her that Tony was the father didn't necessarily make it true.

"You make baskets," he said, as if eager to change the subject.

"We make traditional items to honor our heritage," Halena replied.

"It's what I do for a living," Mary said. For the next twenty minutes as they ate, she told him about Mary's Choctaw Culture Inc., the business that had paid her bills for the last ten years.

In turn he talked about his life and work on the Holiday ranch and it was obvious by his tone that he loved what he did and had a fierce allegiance to Cassie Peterson—big Cass Holiday's niece, who now owned the ranch.

They had just finished eating when Joey cried out from the living room. Tony shot a frantic look at her. It would have been easy for her to take the burden off him and go attend to the little guy, but she met his gaze levelly.

For now they had to function on the assumption that he was the father, and if that was the case, then Tony needed to step up and take responsibility, no matter whether he'd wanted children or not.

"Why don't you go tend to him and I'll clear the dinner dishes," she said.

"And I'm going to write a blog about tornadoes and tin men," Halena announced as she got up from the table and headed out of the room.

Tony looked at Mary curiously. "Don't ask," she said.

It was only when he left the kitchen that Mary realized his presence in the house had her just a bit breathless. It was ridiculous how acutely aware of him she had been while they'd eaten.

He not only had a strong and handsome countenance, but he also had hands that were big and capable, with calluses that proved he was a hard worker.

Halena's outlandish comments during the meal had made him laugh out loud twice and his laughter had been deep and rich, and invited anyone around him to join in.

She finished up in the kitchen and went into the living room. Joey was in the bouncy chair on the floor facing Tony, who sat on the edge of the sofa and dangled a colorful plastic ring of keys in front of the baby.

Joey kicked and waved his hands with a happy smile on his face.

Tony's features held a combination of quiet horror and awe. He looked up and smiled as she entered the room. It was a smile that pooled a touch of unwanted heat in the pit of her stomach.

"Are all babies this happy?" he asked as she sat next to him.

"I'm certainly not an expert on the matter, but yes, I would guess that most babies are naturally happy as long as they have a full tummy and a clean diaper."

She should have sat in the chair across from him. She should have never sat next to him, where she could smell his evocative male scent, where his energy seemed to wrap around her and leave her with that breathless feeling once again.

"I haven't been around any babies before," he said as his focus once again returned to Joey.

"Is there a specific reason why you don't want any children?" she asked.

His eyes immediately shuttered and his shoulders stiffened slightly. He set the plastic keys on the coffee table and then scooted back deeper into the sofa. "It's just a decision I made a long time ago. It's not like I hate kids or anything. I've just never seen myself as a father."

She knew he was one of the cowboys that several not-so-nice people in Bitterroot referred to as the lost boys. They were men who had been hired on when they'd been young teenagers, mere boys who either had been thrown away by their families or had chosen to run away.

She couldn't help but wonder what Tony's story was and then she reminded herself she shouldn't even be interested. Within the next day or two Amy would show up or he'd find her and then she'd never see Tony Nakni again.

Chapter 3

Tony walked out of Mary's front door at just after eight thirty. He'd given the baby a bottle and then he'd changed his diaper and clothes and placed him in the playpen for bed.

Mary accompanied him out to his truck. "What time should we expect you tomorrow evening?"

"About four thirty or five," he replied.

The deep shadows of approaching night clung to her features, emphasizing her straight nose, her high cheekbones and the dark depths of her eyes. God, she was beautiful in moonlight and shadows, he thought.

"We'll hold dinner until you arrive."

"You don't have to do that," he protested. "You're already doing so much for me."

She smiled. "Setting another plate on the table is no big deal."

He shoved his hands in his pockets and stepped back from her. "I don't think your grandmother likes me very much."

Her smile widened. "If she's giving you a hard time, then she likes you. If she isn't speaking to you at all, then you have to worry."

He frowned. "She didn't have a lot to say to me."

"That's because you were interrupting our usual routine. Sunday and Wednesday nights are always movie nights for us, complete with popcorn and theater candy."

"Why didn't you say anything? I could have taken the baby into the bedroom so that you two could have gone about your normal routine."

Once again she smiled at him. "A little shake-up in the routine isn't always a bad thing. Now, you'd better get back to the ranch and we'll see you tomorrow evening." She didn't wait for his reply but instead turned and headed into the house.

He got into his truck and took off for the Holiday ranch with Mary on his mind. She'd smelled of dark and mysterious spices, so different from the light floral scent that Amy had always worn.

He'd cared about Amy and he worried about the trouble she might be in now, but something about Mary Redwing stirred him on a level no woman had ever done before. Amy had been like a delightful teenager, but Mary was definitely all grown-up woman.

And something about her scared him just a little bit. A lick of desire burned in his stomach when he got near her and he couldn't afford to make any mistakes where she was concerned.

Just a couple of days, he reminded himself. He needed her now because he had no other alternative. He was just grateful that she'd agreed to help him out.

Why wasn't she already married? She must be in her early thirties. She was beautiful and was a successful entrepreneur and she even knew how to cook. Why hadn't some man already snapped her up to build a family?

As he turned onto the long Holiday ranch drive that would take him to the shed where the men parked their vehicles, his thoughts shifted back to Amy. Maybe while he'd been gone today she'd come back here. Maybe she was sitting in the cowboy dining room right now just waiting for him to return with Joey.

Although he didn't see her car anywhere it didn't douse the modicum of hope that rose up inside him. She might not be here right at this very moment, but it was possible she'd been here earlier in the afternoon. Hopefully, if she'd been here and gone, she'd spoken to several of the other cowboys and had given somebody a phone number where Tony could contact her.

That hope carried him from the shed to the back of the cowboy motel, where he knew a few of the men would still be up in the recreational area of the large dining room.

Before he even entered, the dulcet tones of Mac McBride's guitar drifting out on the cool night air met his ears. The man could make magic with that musical instrument and he sang as well as he played. Most evenings ended with Mac entertaining the men with a few songs before bedtime.

Mac stopped playing and set his guitar down next to him when Tony entered through the door. Mac wasn't alone in the room. The ranch foreman, Adam Benson, was there, along with Sawyer, Brody and Clay.

"You didn't have to stop playing," Tony protested.

"It's all right. We were about ready to call it a night anyway," Mac replied easily.

"The men told me about the baby," Adam said.

"Yeah, I've arranged with Mary Redwing to watch him during working hours until I get back in touch with Amy. I don't suppose anyone saw her around here today while I was gone?" Tony's heart sank as the men all shook their heads.

"What are you going to do, Tony? How are you going to find Amy?" Sawyer asked.

Tony swept his hat off his head and released a deep sigh. "I'll wait another day or two and then I suppose I might talk to Dillon to see if he has any contacts in Oklahoma City who might help me locate her."

"Aren't you afraid she'll get in trouble if you go to the police?" Sawyer asked.

"She didn't abandon the baby someplace on the street, so there shouldn't be a legal issue," Tony replied. "If I have to, I'll hire a private investigator to help me find her." He eased down in one of the chairs that faced the sofa.

What he wanted right now was just a little male small talk. His head had been filled with women all day long. One woman had pulled forth old bittersweet feelings and the other one had evoked new, exciting feelings that he definitely didn't want.

"Anything new going on around here?" he asked.

"Cassie informed me this morning that she's going to hire on another ranch hand or two," Adam said.

"I hope it's somebody who fits well with all of us," Sawyer replied.

"We could definitely use more help around here," Mac added.

"But it's good news for all of us that she's hiring on somebody," Tony replied. "That implies that she intends to stick around here."

Since the moment the New York artist had taken over the ranch, the fear had been that Cassie would sell it and displace all the men who had called it their home for so many years.

The ranch wasn't just their home—the men had also formed a family unit based on common pasts and a fierce loyalty to each other that had been branded into them by the tough, but loving, Cass Holiday.

"I still can't get a feel for if she intends to stay here forever or eventually sell the place and head back to New York," Adam replied.

"Have you gotten a feel for anything else about her?" Clay asked with a teasing glint in his eyes.

A flush of color rose up in Adam's cheeks. "Cassie and I have a strictly professional relationship."

"Who are you kidding? We all know you have the hots for her. When are you going to get up the nerve and ask her out?" Sawyer asked.

"When I feel like the time is right," Adam replied

curtly. He turned to look at Tony. "Have you spoken to Chief Bowie today?"

"Yeah, I saw him right after noon in the café." A touch of anger stirred in him as he remembered the encounter with the men from the Humes place.

"Did he mention to you that they've identified one of the skeletons that was found here?"

Tony sat up straighter in the chair. "No, in fact I asked him if there was anything new on the case and he told me there wasn't."

"He must have gotten this news after he saw you," Adam replied. "He was here at dinnertime asking if anyone remembered a fifteen-year-old boy named Tim Hankins."

Tony frowned. "We've all told him over and over again that there were no other boys here other than the twelve of us."

"Well, apparently Tim Hankins was here at one time or another, since his bones were found under the shed and his skull was the one Dusty fished out of the pond," Clay replied.

Tony's blood chilled as he remembered the day Dusty had brought his girlfriend, Trisha, and her young son to the pond for a day of fishing fun only to have it tainted by the gruesome catch.

When the bones had initially been dug up and studied by Dr. Patience Forbes, it had been discovered that a skull and finger bones were absent. Dusty had found the skull in the pond, but the finger bones had yet to be found.

"Was he a lost boy, too?" Tony asked.

Adam nodded. "According to Dillon he was a runaway from Tulsa."

"I wonder how he got here from Tulsa," Tony said.

"I wonder who killed him and all those others with an ax or a meat cleaver to the back of their heads," Sawyer replied in a darkly somber tone.

The men were all silent for several long moments and Tony knew they were thinking about the seven boys who had been murdered right here on the property so many years ago.

The worst part of it all was the thread of suspicion that had been planted among the men who had basically grown up together, the men Tony considered his brothers. Everyone knew that Dillon suspected one of them of being the potential killer.

Tony had no idea what the others thought, but he couldn't believe any of the other men who worked on the Holiday ranch were capable of such a heinous act. He definitely didn't want to believe it.

"Did Dillon talk to Francine Rogers about him?" Tony asked. Francine had been a close friend of Cass's and was the social worker who had brought all the boys to the Holiday ranch for a chance at a new life.

"I asked him that and he said Francine has been diagnosed with Alzheimer's and has no real memories or notes from fifteen years ago," Adam replied.

Tony sighed in frustration. Everyone wanted this solved to lift the pall that had settled over the ranch since the skeletons had been found.

"I think it's time for me to call it a night," Adam said and got up from his chair.

"Yeah, me, too. Morning comes early." Mac stood from the sofa and grabbed his guitar.

Clay and Tony followed them out of the building and then Adam locked the door. Cord Cully, aka Cookie, would open the dining room door again in the morning when he came in to fix them all their morning meal.

They talked about chores for the next day as they went around the building and then each of them disappeared into their respective rooms.

Tony walked into his and spied a yellow baby blanket that must have fallen out of the suitcase before he'd packed it up to take it to Mary. It was a bright splash of sunshine against his dark brown bedspread.

He picked it up and then sat on the edge of his bed and thought about the baby who might or might not be his. He couldn't quite believe Amy had gotten pregnant by him, although he supposed she could have lied to him about being on the pill and it wasn't unheard of for a condom to break.

He'd never wanted to be a father, but if Joey was his, then Tony would man up and try to be a decent parent. It was the right thing to do.

What he didn't want was in any way to get attached to him without knowing the truth. Amy could reappear at any moment and confess to him that the baby wasn't his. She could snatch him away and Tony would never see him again.

First thing in the morning he'd make an appointment to take Joey into Dr. Rivers's for a checkup, and while he was there, he'd have the doctor do a DNA test.

The odds were Amy would be back long before the

test results ever came in, but at least Tony would have the peace of mind in knowing the truth.

If he didn't hear anything from Amy by Tuesday night, then first thing Wednesday morning he'd have a talk with Dillon and see if he knew a private investigator who worked the Oklahoma City area.

He folded the baby blanket and placed it next to his hat and his gun and holster on the top of the chest of drawers, then took off his clothes and got into bed.

He stared up at the dark ceiling as his mind worked to process everything that had happened since the night before, when the frantic knock had sounded at his door.

An unusually high level of adrenaline had gotten him through the day and now his body relaxed into the familiar mattress as a wave of exhaustion overtook him.

He closed his eyes and was almost asleep when a disturbing thought stabbed through his brain. He hadn't mentioned Amy's parting words to Mary.

Protect him from evil.

"You are such a happy baby," Mary said to Joey as she changed him into a clean white T-shirt and a pair of tiny jeans. Joey gurgled and cooed and then laughed in response.

Tony had called earlier to tell her that he'd made a four-thirty appointment with Dr. Rivers to give the baby a checkup. It was now four fifteen and she expected Tony to arrive at any moment.

First thing that morning Mary had gotten on her computer and printed off a sample sleep-and-feeding schedule for a three-month-old. None of them knew for sure exactly how old Joey was, but according to everything she had read he was doing things that a three- to four-month-old would do.

Halena had laughed at her for needing a piece of paper to take care of a baby, but Mary hadn't been around many babies before and certainly had never been in charge of one. Even though this was a temporary arrangement, she didn't want to screw things up.

She scooped up Joey from her bed and went into the kitchen, where Halena was on dinner duty for the night. Ground beef, onions and spices simmered in a skillet. "Hmm, something smells good."

"Enchilada pie and it will be ready around five thirty," Halena said and picked up a wooden spoon to stir the meat.

"That should be perfect," Mary replied. "Tony should be back from the appointment by then." She was unsurprised by Halena's choice of a dish. Halena loved Mexican food as much as she loved action movies, and on the nights she cooked, the fare was always from south of the border.

A knock sounded on the door. "That should be Tony," Mary said. Just knowing she was going to see him danced a bit of shimmering light through her, a light she didn't want to shine at all.

She opened the door and Joey laughed and leaned out of her arms toward him. "Whoa," she said and tightened her grip around his sturdy little body. "Hi, Tony. I know you need to get to the doctor's office. The car seat is in the spare room if you want to get it."

"I'll just go grab it." He swept by her and she caught

the scent of minty soap and the pleasant cologne she'd noticed the day before.

He returned with the car seat in hand. "I'll carry him out," she said.

He stared at her, his dark eyes radiating both surprise and a touch of alarm. "You aren't coming with me?"

"I hadn't planned on it. Tony, I'm just the babysitter," she reminded him.

"Of course," he replied.

She carried Joey out to his truck, where he secured the car seat in the back of the king cab. "You'll be fine," she said as she handed Joey to him and watched as he buckled in the boy. "And dinner will be ready when you get back here. I hope you like Mexican. Grandmother made an enchilada pie."

He nodded. "Sounds terrific. I'll see you in a little while." He got into the truck and pulled out of the driveway.

"It was a good decision for you not to go," Halena said when Mary returned to the house. "It's important for you to remember your place in all this."

"I know." Mary sank down in a chair at the table. "But it's difficult to maintain distance when Joey is so beautiful and happy and obviously bright."

"And he'll be gone before too long."

Mary eyed her grandmother with a touch of amusement. "But didn't I see you leaning over his playpen at nap time whispering to him?"

Halena frowned. "You shouldn't be spying on an old woman."

Mary laughed and then sobered. "Don't worry, I'm

very aware that this is all temporary. In a couple of days things will be back to normal."

Halena grinned at her, the familiar wicked twinkle in her eyes. "*Normal* has never had a place in our home."

Mary laughed again and then together they made a big salad to go with the evening meal. Talk of Tony and the baby was replaced by conversation about the craft fair that was approaching far too quickly.

It was five fifteen when there was a knock at the door once again. Tony was back and Joey was asleep in the car seat. "He got a clean bill of health," he said in obvious relief. "And I had Dr. Rivers do a paternity test."

"How long does it take to get the results back?" Mary asked. How she wished being in his presence didn't free more than a few butterflies to whirl around in her stomach. This whole arrangement would be easier if she didn't find Tony so darned attractive.

"Four to six weeks," he replied. "No matter what happens with Amy, I need to know if I'm his father."

"Of course you do. Now, come into the kitchen. Grandmother has dinner ready to go on the table."

He followed her into the kitchen, where Halena already sat in her chair. "I can tell by the light in your eyes that things went well at the doctor's," she said to Tony. "I could have told you there was nothing wrong with that child. His eyes are clear and his spirit is eager to embrace life."

Tony nodded and sat down. "Dr. Rivers assured me of the same thing."

Halena nodded. "The leaves on the trees told me

the baby was fine. The tree leaves often tell me important things."

Tony nodded and shot a quick, uncertain glance at Mary. She simply smiled. If he was around for any length of time, then he would quickly learn Halena's quirks.

He eyed the food on the table. "It looks like Mary isn't the only one who knows her way around a kitchen. Everything looks delicious."

"Praise will get you nowhere with me," Halena replied, but Mary could tell her grandmother was pleased.

What pleased Halena even more was that Tony was a movie buff, too. He told them that sometimes in the evenings the men at the ranch all gathered in the recreation room and watched DVDs until bedtime.

Mary listened in amusement as the two talked about failed plots, silly characters and unrealistic action scenes in some of the movies they'd both watched.

For the first time she saw Tony completely animated. The spark in his eyes and the wide smile that curved his lips drew her in. She shouldn't enjoy looking at him so much, and she definitely shouldn't be enjoying his company.

"Those kick-butt heroines they have in some of the movies today don't have anything over this old woman," Halena said. "I can use my broom as a lethal weapon against marauding raccoons and other wild animals. My shotgun stays next to my bed and I can hit anything I aim at."

She turned to look at Mary. "Maybe I need to get

me a pair of those stiletto heels that actresses wear in the movies."

Mary looked at her in horror. "I'm not sure that's a great idea, Grandmother. You rock your flip-flops and tennis shoes just fine."

Halena lifted her chin proudly. "I rock everything I wear just fine."

Dinner finished and, as if on cue, Joey cried out, ready for his bottle. While Mary cleaned up the dishes, Tony prepared a bottle and went into the living room and Halena went to her room to write her evening blog.

It would be easy to fall into a crazy fantasy of a strong, handsome male taking care of the baby in the evenings while Mary attended to the dinner dishes.

It would be far too easy to imagine the two of them tucking the baby into bed for the night and then going into their own bedroom to make love and sleep in each other's arms.

Once upon a time Mary had entertained those kinds of dreams, but over the years they had been stolen from her by a ravaging disease and bitter life experiences.

She couldn't fall into any sort of romantic fantasies. It would be foolish, and Mary was no fool. She knew who and what she was and it was nothing any man would ever want.

When she went into the living room, Tony had finished with the bottle and Joey was ready for a little playtime. She took the blanket from the back of the sofa and spread it on the floor and then put the boy down with a few of his toys in front of him.

"He doesn't seem to miss Amy," Tony said. Joey

raised his head and looked at Tony, then grinned and released a string of jabber along with a bit of drool.

"He also seems to have bonded pretty quickly to you." She sat down next to him on the sofa. "What made you decide you didn't want children?" she asked curiously. He was a young, vital man who appeared to have all the qualities that would make a wonderful father.

"I don't want to get married. That's one reason why I never wanted kids. I also didn't have a father when I was growing up, so I had no role model to know how to do it right. What about you? Are you close to your parents?"

She had a feeling he'd changed the focus from him to her intentionally. "My mother died of breast cancer when I was eight and then my father was killed in a car accident when I was nine. Halena raised me and she's been like a mother and a father to me."

"And now you're raising her," he replied.

She laughed. "Don't let her hear you say that." She sobered. "It's the way it's supposed to be. Our parents teach us to use a spoon to eat and how to walk and as they age into their twilight years it's our turn to help them use a spoon and to walk. It's a circle of love."

He gazed back at Joey, a muscle ticking in his strong jawline. "He's so small and helpless."

"He's like a blank page waiting to be written on," she said softly. "If you're his father, then what will you write in his book of life?"

Before he could reply, Halena came into the room and Joey fell back asleep for a quick nap. The rest of the evening passed quickly as Halena took center stage and entertained Tony with stories about her interactions with her blog readers.

"People just get crazy when they go on social media," she said. "They post pictures and say things they'd never talk about in real life. It's quite a strange phenomenon."

"I don't do social media," Tony replied. "I don't think any of us men at the ranch even own one of those smartphones. As far as I'm concerned, my phone is for calls and nothing else." He frowned. "I wonder if Amy does social media."

"She used to have a Facebook page," Mary replied. She got up from the sofa and grabbed her laptop from the top of the nearby small desk. She sat back down next to Tony and powered it on.

As she logged in, he scooted closer to her side, so close that his thigh pressed against hers, so close that her heartbeat quickened and once again she felt as if she wasn't getting quite enough oxygen.

"Hopefully she's posted something that will give us some answers as to where she might be now," he said.

Mary clicked on the site and then pulled up Amy's page. There was the familiar picture of her friend, but there was also a notice that if she wanted to see any personal information about Amy she had to send a friend request.

"She must have unfriended me at some point in time," Mary said with a sigh of disappointment.

"Why would she do that?" he asked, obvious frustration in his voice.

Mary shut down her computer and rose once again, needing to distance herself from his intimate proximity.

"She's done it before in the past. Whenever she goes off the deep end and starts using drugs again, she cuts off all contact with me."

"Amy is by nature a people pleaser, and when she is doing things she knows Mary disapproves of, she hides," Halena said.

Tony stared down at Joey. "She told me to protect him from evil."

"Perhaps that evil is Amy herself," Mary replied.

"Drugs are the real evil that destroys people's lives," Halena replied. "She brought him to you because she obviously knew she wasn't fit to have him."

"What am I going to do if she's never fit, if she's never in a place to be a healthy mother to him?" Tony looked at Halena and then at Mary.

"Then you have to be the rock in his life. No matter what your feelings were about having children before, you have to step up and embrace your fatherhood," Halena said as she stood from the chair. "A good warrior takes care of what is his. You have the beautiful hair of a warrior, but the real question is do you have a warrior's heart? Now, I'm going to bed."

"Grandmother sometimes speaks in lectures," Mary said once Halena had left the room.

"It's okay," he assured her. "So did Cass Holiday. She used to say even grown men needed a lecture from a woman every once in a while."

"You miss her," she said. She sank down in the chair Halena had vacated.

"We all do. She was the mother none of us had ever had."

She wanted to ask him more questions. She'd like to know how he had come to be on the Holiday ranch, where his mother and father were and so much more. But he stood abruptly.

"It's getting late. I should probably head back to the ranch. Do you want me to give Joey another bottle or change him or anything before I go?"

I'd like you to kiss me before you leave. The inappropriate thought stunned her as it unexpectedly leaped into her brain. She jumped up from the chair. "No, we're fine. I can take it from here."

She suddenly wanted him gone. He needed to take his gorgeous self away from her. She didn't want to smell the clean male scent of him, she didn't want to fall into the depths of his beautiful dark eyes.

This whole situation was crazy and something about Tony Nakni was making her more than just a little bit crazy. She walked him to the door, and when they reached it, he turned back to look at her. "Mary, I have to confess, I'm enjoying this time in your home."

His gaze held a spark of something forbidden, a heat that beckoned her to move closer to him. She consciously took a step backward. "That's nice. Good night, Tony. I'll see you tomorrow."

Whatever she'd seen in his eyes vanished, making her wonder if she'd really seen it at all. "Okay, then I'll see you tomorrow evening," he replied.

She released a deep sigh and closed the door behind him. She leaned her head against the wood, momentarily overwhelmed with a piercing grief that felt new and raw even though she'd been through it before.

You will never be a wife and you'll never be a mother. Never again will you enjoy being held in a man's arms and being kissed until you're mindless. You can't even be a man's hit-it-and-quit-it kind of fling.

The painful inner voice whispered the words to her, reminding her that even though there had been a hint of desire for her in Tony's eyes, she would never be anything to him except a temporary babysitter. She would never be anything to any man.

She was simply too damaged to repair.

Chapter 4

Tony sat on the back of his horse and waved to Flint on horseback in the distance. Low clouds hung overhead and the cattle were uneasy, as if anticipating the threat of a late-afternoon autumn storm.

The weather and the animals mirrored Tony's restless and unsettled mood. The continued absence of Amy made him unsettled and his intense attraction to Mary definitely made him restless.

He wanted to keep his distance from Joey, but the baby had the face and the happy disposition of a toothless angel. Still, the last thing he wanted to do was love the baby only for Amy to return and confess that Joey wasn't his.

Tony didn't want to bond with the baby and then have the real father come out of the shadows and take him away. Other than Cass being taken by a force of nature he hadn't been able to control, he didn't put himself in positions where he'd suffer a loss.

Tony was the one who always walked away. In the few adult relationships he'd had with women, when he sensed the expectations were getting too big, when he believed his heart or the woman's heart might be getting involved, that was when he walked and never looked back.

Still, he'd wanted to kiss Mary the other night. He'd wanted to kiss her desperately, hungrily, but it hadn't happened. He thought he'd sensed desire in her as the evening had wound down, but he wasn't sure and he didn't want to make a mistake where she was concerned. Last night he'd scooted out of her house before he could do anything foolish.

He needed her. He needed the arrangement he'd made with her and the last thing he wanted to do was screw up things. He gave the reins a flick and headed toward the stable.

It was time to call it a day here and head to Mary's. Tonight was movie night and he planned to stop in town on the way to her place and pick up some microwave popcorn and candy. He was certain the gesture would please Halena. What he couldn't figure out was why he even wanted to please the old woman.

When he rode into the stable, Brody was inside brushing down his horse. "Feels like it's going to storm," Tony said as he dismounted.

"We could use whatever rain we get." Brody guided

his horse into a stall and then turned to look at Tony. "We've missed you at dinner the last couple of nights."

"I feel like I'm living a double life right now," he admitted as he pulled off the saddle.

"By day a rough-and-tumble cowboy and by night a daddy in distress. Better you than me, my man," Brody said with a dry laugh.

"It's not all bad," Tony replied. "Joey is a good baby, I'm eating great dinners and I'm in the company of a beautiful woman."

"Right, and her crazy grandma."

"Halena is definitely interesting," Tony replied with a small laugh. "But this arrangement with Mary isn't going to last forever. Tomorrow I'm contacting Dillon to see if he knows somebody in Oklahoma City who might be able to find Amy."

"What are you going to do? Find her and then drag her back kicking and screaming and make her be a mother?" Brody's eyes flashed darkly. "A woman who abandons her kid shouldn't be found. You, of all people, should know that, Tony."

"I just need to find out what's going on in her life and if she needs help," Tony replied.

"You can't help somebody who doesn't want your help."

Tony sighed with a touch of frustration. "Are you trying to depress me on purpose?"

Brody gave him a wry grin. "You know me, I'm the hard-nosed realist in the group. And now I'm heading in for a shower and some dinner. I heard Cookie made his famous chili tonight."

Tony watched the tall, dark-haired man leave the stables. Brody was the resident hard-ass and pessimist. In all the years that the men had worked for Cass, he'd never shared any details about what had driven him to be living on the streets at the age of fifteen.

Of course, Tony hadn't shared many of the horrors of his own childhood with any of the other men. There were some things you just didn't speak of, wicked things that had scarred the heart too deeply for mere words.

By five o'clock he was on his way to Mary's place. He'd stopped and picked up the goodies for movie night and was surprised by how much he looked forward to the evening.

Mary greeted him at the door and looked lovelier than he'd ever seen her. Instead of her hair being braided down her back, it was a long curtain of darkness around her shoulders that made his fingers itch with the desire to lose themselves in it.

"I come bearing movie-night gifts," he said and thrust the paper bag he carried into her arms. "There's microwave popcorn with extra butter and chewy candy, crunchy chocolate and licorice."

"You didn't have to do that," she replied and took the bag from him.

"It's the very least I could do." He followed her through the living room, where Joey was asleep in his bouncy chair, and into the kitchen. There was no sign of Halena.

Mary motioned him to sit at the table. "I guess you still haven't heard anything from Amy." She began to unload the bag.

"Nothing. I had intended to call Dillon this morning to see if he could help, but I didn't get a chance. Both Mac and Sawyer woke up with stomach-flu symptoms and so we were a bit shorthanded for the daily chores."

"I hope they feel better. Maybe you should call Dillon after dinner tonight." Mary turned from the counter to look at him, her expression unreadable.

"I'll do that," he said. He had to remember that he and Joey were a disruption to her life and he needed to either find Amy, or make different arrangements for the baby sooner rather than later. "I know there's a day-care center in town. Maybe I should check in to them watching Joey during the day."

She frowned. "That means you'll have him in the bunkhouse during the nights. That doesn't sound like a great idea. I'm good having him here for a while longer, Tony. Hopefully Dillon will be able to find Amy and then whatever arrangements you make for Joey will be between her and you."

And then he'd have no more reason to see Mary anymore. He was surprised that the thought depressed him a bit. The past few nights of spending time in her home had been far more pleasant than he'd ever anticipated.

There was a calm quiet about her that he found attractive. There was a peace in the air that surrounded her, a serenity that called to something deep inside him.

He couldn't deny that he was intensely attracted to her, but she had given him little indication that she might return the feeling.

Joey cried out from the living room and Tony jumped

up to attend to him. He unbuckled him from his seat and pulled him into his arms.

Joey immediately stopped fussing and instead gazed at Tony for a long moment and then smiled, a rivulet of drool sneaking down his chin.

What will you write in his book of life?

An unexpected fierce protectiveness swelled up inside Tony. It was a feeling he'd never experienced before. A lump formed in the back of his throat as he stared into Joey's bright eyes.

One thing was for certain—nobody would scribble the vile ugliness in this child that had been written in Tony's book of life.

Ash stared out his car window. He was parked down the street from the beige house where his child was inside. It had taken him two days of following the cowboy from the Holiday ranch to this home to confirm that little Joey was in there.

He wouldn't be there for long.

Ash and his men had yet to locate Amy. At the moment she was the last thing on his mind. All he cared about at this moment was getting his kid back where he belonged. Joey was his and nobody took what was Ash's.

In the two days he'd been watching the house he hadn't seen any man present other than the cowboy, who came every evening and left around twilight. He'd seen the old woman and the younger one, but no man.

There also didn't appear to be any alarm system at

the house. All of that was going to make it so much easier for Ash to get what was his.

He tightened his hands around the steering wheel. He'd prefer to get in and get Joey without anyone getting hurt, but he'd do whatever it took to get his boy back.

Tonight Joey would sleep in his own crib, in Ash's home. And when he finally found Joey's mother, she was a dead woman.

Tony called Dillon just after dinner and the lawman arrived at Mary's house twenty minutes later. She invited him into the living room, where Tony and Halena sat on the sofa with Joey once again in his bouncy chair.

"Halena, have you been behaving yourself?" Dillon asked as he eased down in the chair across from them.

"No, but you know I try not to break too many laws when I do misbehave," she replied.

Dillon grinned, but his smile lasted only a moment as he gazed at the baby and then at Tony. "So, what's going on and what can I do to help you?"

Mary listened as Tony related Amy's sudden appearance at the bunkhouse on Sunday night. "She dropped off the baby and drove away. I definitely think she's in some kind of trouble and I just wondered if you had any suggestions on how I can find her," Tony said.

Dillon frowned. "Last I heard anything about her, she'd moved from here to Oklahoma City. I haven't heard anything about her since then."

"That's all we know, too. I thought maybe you'd know somebody on the police department there who could look for her," Tony said.

"No police are going to get involved in what appears to be a domestic issue. As far as we know, she hasn't broken any laws. She left the baby with you and said that you're the father. Unfortunately in this kind of a situation it isn't against the law for a mother to walk away," Dillon replied.

"So, if the police won't get involved, do you know a good private investigator who might be able to help?" There was a quiet despair in Tony's voice. "I'd at least like to know that she's okay."

Was he still in love with Amy? It was certainly possible, and if he was, what difference did it make to her? Mary knew she was just a convenience to him at the moment and nothing more. She shouldn't want to be any more to him.

"I do know a private investigator who might be able to help you," Dillon said, pulling her out of her crazy thoughts. "His name is Mick Blake." Dillon took his cell phone out of his pocket. "I've got his number here someplace." Dillon found the number and Tony put it into his cell phone.

"Mick is a good guy and is one of the best private investigators I've ever run across," Dillon added.

"Are you all done now?" Halena asked, not hiding her impatience. "We have movies to watch and popcorn to pop."

Dillon rose. "I'm sorry, Tony. I can't do much of anything to help you. Hopefully, Mick can locate Amy for you and you'll get the answers you need."

Tony got up as well and walked the lawman to the front door. "I'll give Mick a call. I appreciate your time,

Dillon. I know you have a lot of other things on your plate."

Minutes later Tony returned to his seat on the sofa next to Halena and Mary went into the kitchen to fix the popcorn. A rumble of thunder accompanied the microwave popping.

Apparently, the storm that had threatened all day was moving in. Mary hated gray skies and thunderstorms. Every loss she'd ever suffered in her life had been accompanied by rain.

She had vague memories of rain pattering against a hospital window when she said her last goodbye to her mother. It had been in a rainstorm that her father had suffered his fatal car accident.

There had been more rain in her lifetime, and more losses…too many losses.

"Before the movie starts, I should tell you the rules of movie night," Halena said to Tony when Mary entered the room with a big bowl of the buttery treat.

"Rules?" Tony looked at the old woman quizzically.

Halena nodded. "We don't talk through the show. We pause it for bathroom breaks and that's when, if you really feel the need to chatter, you can."

"Got it," Tony replied, his eyes lighting up with amusement.

Oh, the man was positively killing her, Mary thought as she placed the bowl of popcorn in the center of the table. When he smiled, when that twinkle appeared in his eyes, she wanted nothing more than to fall into his big, strong arms.

It had been years since she'd felt this way about a

man. And the last time she had, it had ended so badly that she'd been left ashamed and humiliated, and with anger at the universe burning in her heart. She hadn't even thought of getting close to any man since then.

She snapped her focus to the television, where Halena had started the movie. Through the next two hours Tony attended to Joey's needs and appeared to enjoy the show as outside lightning slashed the sky, thunder rumbled overhead and the rain came down in torrents.

His gaze caught hers several times throughout and she saw a soft heat in his eyes. It was the same kind of heat she'd seen there when he'd been about to leave two nights before…when she thought he might kiss her.

The storm shot a restlessness through her and his heated looks did nothing to calm the edge of anxiety. The last thing she wanted or needed was any personal relationship between them.

Halena broke the movie-night rules dozens of times throughout the movie, yelling at the television, shouting words of encouragement to the hero and pausing it three times simply to talk about the action. And each time Tony grinned at Mary with that darned twinkle in his eyes.

By the time the movie was over, she was ready for Tony to leave.

The rain had eased to a soft pitter-patter and the thunder had stilled by the time he was ready to go. "Walk me to the door?" he asked.

She nodded and then bent down and scooped Joey off the blanket, where he'd been rolling around and exploring his bare toes. The baby in her arms was her safety net, a physical barrier that she hoped would keep her wistful wish for a kiss from Tony at bay.

They reached the front door and he gazed at her somberly. "I'll call the private detective first thing in the morning, but in the meantime maybe I should check out of the cowboy motel on the ranch and get an apartment someplace. I promised you this arrangement would only last a couple of days."

"Tony, please don't do anything rash," she protested.

"If I had an apartment, then I could put him in day care and then have a nice place to keep him overnight."

"I'm good with the arrangement we have right now." She tightened her arms around Joey. "And I'll give you a heads-up when it's not okay with me."

"You promise?" His dark gaze held hers intently.

"I promise," she replied.

He reached out a hand and her heart stopped in her chest as she anticipated his touch, but he stroked a finger down Joey's cheek, making him wiggle and coo. He dropped his hand back to his side.

"Maybe by tomorrow night the private investigator will have some news for me."

"It would be nice to have some answers," she replied. "We'll see you tomorrow night."

He nodded and went out into the night.

She closed and locked the door and then returned to the living room, where Halena sat on the sofa. "I'm just going to give Joey his bottle and then tuck him into bed." She went into the kitchen and then returned a moment later and began to feed Joey.

"You like him," Halena said.

Mary smiled at her. "Don't you?"

"I like some things about him, but my final verdict is still out."

"It really doesn't matter whether we like him or not. He's only going to be around until he can sort out this mess," Mary replied.

"He looks at you with lust in his eyes."

Mary couldn't help the quickened thump of her heartbeat at her grandmother's words. She forced a light laugh. "He'll get over it."

"And will you?" Halena's dark gaze bore into her.

"I don't feel that way about him," she replied.

"And tomorrow I might wear a live chicken on my head," Halena retorted. Mary laughed and her grandmother raised her chin. "It could happen," she added and got up from the sofa. "And now I'm going to bed."

"It's still early," Mary said.

"It seems lately I only sleep in fits and starts. For the last two nights I've gotten up at two to check my blog. I'm hoping I can catch up on some sleep tonight."

"Good night, Grandmother," Mary said.

"Good night, my granddaughter. May you dream-walk only to happy places." Halena left the room.

Mary finished feeding Joey and then carried him into her bedroom, where she changed his diaper and put him into a pair of pajamas.

She then took him into the spare room and placed him in the playpen. He had yet to cry when she put him down for a nap or for the night. She leaned over and rubbed his back and he wiggled around for a moment, then closed his eyes. Within minutes he was sound asleep.

Mary went back into her own bedroom and got ready for bed. As she took off her clothes, she turned her back to the dresser mirror. She never looked at her reflection when she was naked. She hated the woman in the mirror.

She pulled on an oversize T-shirt and then crawled into her bed. Like Halena, for the past couple of nights Mary had battled with a bit of insomnia.

She didn't have to look far to find what caused her restless sleep. Each night thoughts of Tony and Joey filled her head. They were forbidden thoughts of family and love and created an ache inside her that kept sleep at bay.

After a while, she felt she must have fallen asleep, because she awakened to Halena yelling from the kitchen. What was going on? Had Halena suffered another heart attack?

Her heart crashed against her ribs as she jumped out of bed. She ran down the hallway, through the living room and into the kitchen to see her grandmother, clad in a short hot-pink nightgown with orange-striped sleep pants beneath, running out onto the porch with her shotgun in her hands.

"Come back here, you stinking thief—come back here and let me fill your black heart with buckshot," she yelled into the darkness of the night.

"Call Chief Bowie," she said to Mary over her shoulder. "A shadow being tried to enter our home tonight."

A shadow being…an evil entity.

A deep chill swept through Mary as she heard the unmistakable fear trembling in her grandmother's voice.

Chapter 5

"You missed all the excitement here last night," Mary said to Tony the next evening as he gave Joey a bottle. It was just the two of them in the room as Halena had disappeared into her bedroom right after dinner.

"Excitement?" He gazed at her expectantly. He'd been in a state of simmering excitement since the day he'd appeared on her doorstep. There was just something about Mary that enticed him, that delighted him.

"We had a break-in at two thirty in the morning," she replied.

"A break-in?" He sat up straighter, unconsciously pulling the bottle nipple from Joey's mouth. Joey fussed a complaint and Tony rectified the problem as he continued to stare at Mary. "What happened?"

"Whoever it was slit a screen on the back porch and

got inside and then broke a pane of glass in the kitchen door. Thankfully, Grandmother heard the tinkle of glass and grabbed her shotgun. Before he could get into the house she confronted him and he turned and ran."

"Did you call Dillon?" He was horrified that any danger might have come close to anyone in this house.

She nodded, her hair rippling like black silk. "He came out and we made a report, although it's doubtful he'll find the person responsible. Grandmother didn't get a good look at him. It was too dark and she said he had on dark clothes and a ski mask."

"Why would somebody break in here?" A sense of alarm still rang inside him. They were two women all alone in this house.

"Dillon speculated that it was possible the person wanted to steal some of my baskets and other things. The craft fair is coming up and lots of people around here know this house fills up with items we intend to sell."

"Would it be worth a thief taking such a chance?"

She smiled at him, that warm, beautiful smile that made the blood in his veins heat with a torturous desire. "You obviously don't know the worth of my baskets. People love them because they're made by a full-blooded Choctaw and because I use the traditional river-cane reed. My pottery brings even bigger prices. So, to answer your question, yes, it would be worth it to somebody to steal from us."

"Have you ever thought about a security system?" He wished he'd been here. He would have chased after the thief and gladly turned him over to Dillon for charges to be pressed.

"Never," she replied. "But we've never had an attempted break-in before. Besides, an alarm probably isn't a good idea. Grandmother would have it ringing ten times a day and through half the night because she would forget how to disarm and rearm it again."

Her eyes lit with humor. "And I don't think our thief will be back. I'm sure he didn't expect to be met by a crazy old Native American woman wielding her shotgun and a very sharp tongue."

"Mary, it isn't funny," Tony replied. "What would have happened if Halena hadn't awakened when she did?"

"I imagine he'd come inside, take what he wanted and then leave. There have been lots of break-ins in this area and so far nobody has gotten hurt."

Tony was vaguely surprised to realize that the surge of protectiveness he'd felt for Joey was also there for Mary and her grandmother.

"Don't look so concerned, Tony. I had both the screen and the door window fixed today and I really don't think he'll be back. Now, you mentioned at dinner that you'd contacted Mick Blake about finding Amy?"

"Yeah, but unfortunately there wasn't much information I could give him about her to help in the search. I don't have an address for her and I don't know if she had a job or not. If she was living with somebody else, then it's possible she's been off the grid completely. I did tell him the make and model of her car, but that's pretty much the only clues I could give him and that will only help if she's still driving the same vehicle."

Joey finished his bottle. Tony set it on the coffee table in front of him but continued to hold Joey in his arms. His little body snuggled against Tony's chest and he smelled of a sweet scent that Tony could only identify as baby innocence and unconditional love…something Tony had never known in his life.

"Did Mick think he could find her in spite of the lack of any real information?" Mary asked, pulling him from his momentary reverie.

"He was optimistic that he could get me results but cautioned me that it might take some time." He placed the now sleeping baby into the bouncy chair and strapped him in. He stroked a finger down the little boy's plump cheek. He sat back up and gazed at Mary.

"You're falling in love with him," she said.

Tony looked at her in surprise. Was that what it was? The softening of his heart when he looked at Joey? The swell of his chest when Joey smiled at him? Was it possible that Joey had pulled forth a love that Tony hadn't believed he was capable of possessing?

No, it couldn't possibly be love. He'd vowed to himself that Joey wouldn't get into his heart. Tony didn't know how to love. He'd never had any love in his life, except from Cass, and her death had been a huge loss.

"I don't love that easily," he replied. "But I'll admit he is a cutie."

Tony didn't love easily, but he definitely had a deep lust going on for the woman seated next to him on the sofa. She looked so gorgeous this evening, clad in jeans and a pale pink T-shirt that enhanced the dark richness of her hair and her beautiful long-lashed eyes.

"Why aren't you married?" he asked.

Her cheeks flushed with a touch of color. "There are some women who are meant to be married and have a family. I just happen not to be one of those women."

"Why not? You're a beautiful, successful woman."

"I'm happy alone. I have my work and Grandmother's company and that's enough for me." She said the words firmly, but he didn't quite believe them. "Why did you make the decision never to have a wife?"

"I love my horse—that's the cowboy way and that's enough for me," he replied lightly.

She frowned at him. "I'm just trying to get to know you better, Tony. You blew into my life so unexpectedly and at least for now we're bonded together by trying to do what's best for Joey."

There were some things she didn't need to know... some things he just didn't share with anyone. "Mary, what you've seen of me the last four nights is who I am. I'm not that complicated."

Her beautiful eyes bore into his. "If you say so," she replied, but he could tell she didn't believe him. "So, tell me what happened on that ranch of yours today."

"Have you heard that one of the skeletons has been identified?" he asked.

"No," she replied, her eyes widening. "I haven't been in town to hear any of the newest local gossip."

Tony told her about Tim Hankins, the murdered runaway boy who nobody on the ranch knew anything about. When he was finished, he looked down at Joey and once again a wealth of protectiveness rose up inside him.

"If I have any part in raising him, I'll make sure he never has a reason to run away from home," he said.

"You were a runaway when you came to the ranch to work?" she asked, although he figured she already knew the answer to the question.

"Yeah, I had a pretty crummy family life and so when I was almost fifteen I hit the streets, and now it's probably time for me to get home." That was as much as he intended to share and now he felt the need to escape from her and any more questions she might have.

Her gaze was too soft and she was far too easy to talk to. Everything about her drew him in. He wanted to know what she was thinking, what she was feeling, and more than anything he wanted to know what her full lips would taste like beneath his own.

He got up from the sofa and she did the same. Together they walked to the front door. When he turned to tell her goodbye, she stood far too close to him and her lips were parted in a way that shot rational thought right out of his head.

Without giving her any advance warning, he threw an arm around her waist, pulled her tightly against him and then covered her mouth with his.

She released a small gasp, but she didn't step back from him and, rather than telling him no, she opened her lips to him and responded.

Fire danced through his veins. Her lips were soft and warm and they only increased Tony's appetite for more. Her breasts pushed against his chest and the heady scent of her surrounded him. The kiss went on for several long moments and then she broke it and stepped back from him.

The flames of his own desire shot out of her eyes, letting him know that she'd been as moved by the kiss as he had. "That wasn't really a good idea," she said, her voice slightly husky.

He grinned at her. "It wasn't really a bad idea." He reached out and tucked a strand of her long hair behind her ear, his fingers noting the silky softness.

"Tony, it wouldn't be wise for us to indulge in any kind of a relationship other than what we have right now." She took a step back from him.

"Do we always have to be wise?" he countered.

"I try to be," she replied. Joey cried out from behind them. "I need to get him. Good night, Tony."

The dismissal was evident in the firmness of her tone. He murmured a good-night and then headed for his truck. Moments later his headlights slashed through the darkness of the night as he drove toward the Holiday ranch.

On the surface, he and Mary seemed perfect for each other. Neither of them wanted marriage, and if he was to judge by her response to his kiss, then she was as attracted to him as he was to her.

He didn't see how having an intimate relationship with her would in any way screw up things between them. They were both adults and seemed to be on the same page. Even thinking about making love to Mary had him half-aroused.

He rolled down his window to allow in the brisk

night air to cool him down. He'd always believed that he found his peace sitting outside his bunk room or in the recreational area in the back of the cowboy motel.

But these nights shared in Mary and Halena's company had filled him with a new kind of peace, one he'd never felt before. It was because her home was filled with love.

A chill walked up his spine as he thought of the break-in that had occurred the night before. She'd made light of it, but the whole thing concerned him.

Had it really been an attempted robbery? What else could it have been? Would the man come back to try again? Certainly there was plenty of merchandise inside the house that could be sold in places where it could never be tracked. Tony could only hope that a shotgun-wielding Halena had really scared the hell out of the man and he'd never return.

He rolled up his window and fought against a sense of deep foreboding. He had no idea where it came from or what it meant. He just knew that his senses were whispering to him that something bad was going to happen.

He'd felt this same way right before the cowboys had found Cass Holiday's broken body on the lawn between the big house and the cowboy motel after the tornado.

The only thing the men could figure out was that she had been on her way to warn them about the impending storm, when it suddenly hit and sent a large tree branch at her that struck her in the head.

She'd died trying to protect them.

Had Tony brought danger to Mary's house? He

couldn't imagine how her watching Joey could put her at risk. No, it had to have been a simple attempted robbery. Nothing else made any sense, but he also couldn't fathom why he now felt that some sort of darkness was growing near, a darkness that would change them all forever.

"I'm heading out," Halena announced the following Wednesday night.

Mary and Tony sat side by side on the sofa and Mary looked at her grandmother in surprise. "Heading out? Where are you going?"

"You're leaving us on movie night?" Tony asked incredulously.

"Mabel just called and invited me to her home for a night of movies. She's been so lonely since her husband died that I just couldn't tell her no," Halena replied. "The poor thing just needs a little company."

"That's nice," Tony said.

"Her husband has been dead for four years and last time I saw her she was in great spirits," Mary said drily. "Tell the truth, you two are going to the casino."

"How do you know that?" Halena asked.

Mary laughed. "Grandmother, you have on your lucky casino blouse." It was the ugliest blouse Mary had ever seen. The vivid blue had faded over the years and the huge sequined parrot on the front appeared to be smirking.

"Okay, we might stop into the casino for a few minutes," Halena confessed.

"Last time you were stopping in for a few minutes you didn't get home until after three in the morning."

"And I suggest you don't wait up for me tonight," Halena retorted. "I think it's going to be a lucky night." She then moved to the front door. "And Mabel just pulled into the driveway."

"Good luck," Tony yelled as she flew out the door. He turned to Mary and grinned. "That was her lucky blouse?"

"Awful, right? It was given to her by one of her friends and the first time she wore it she went to the casino and won a little jackpot, so now it's her lucky blouse."

"Does she gamble a lot?"

"Not really. She seems to go in spurts. She'll stay away for a long time and then go two or three times a week for a month or so." She bent down and picked up Joey, who had awakened from his short nap and was now ready to interact. She placed him in her lap so he faced Tony and the little boy pumped his legs and arms with delight.

"Hi, Joey," Tony said. "Did you have a nice sleep?"

Joey responded with a string of coos and grins. Mary's heart swelled. Over the last couple of days it had been wonderful to see the growing relationship between Tony and the baby.

And over the last few days it had been impossible to ignore the simmer of desire that was like another person in the room whenever she and Tony were together.

The kiss they'd shared had haunted her. It had been years since she'd had a man's warm lips against her own and tasted the sweet hot fire of desire. Tony Nakni definitely knew how to kiss.

She wanted him to kiss her again, and that was definitely foolish. A kiss was a promise of something more to come and she could never deliver on that particular promise.

Still, she wanted Tony and that want filled her with both a wild exhilaration and a bitterness that she'd thought she'd left behind her.

"Are you all ready for the craft fair?" he asked.

"As ready as we can be. I've rented a truck to take everything to the fairgrounds around dawn on Friday morning and we'll be open for business by nine thirty. You're coming on Saturday?"

"Actually, I talked to Adam and got my work schedule shifted around so I could be there all day on Friday, Saturday and Sunday." He smiled at her. "I figured maybe you could use a carnival barker and a babysitter while you and Halena work."

"Thank you. That would be terrific and we could definitely use your help with Joey. Now, how about I make us some after-dinner coffee?"

"Sounds good."

She stood and plopped Joey into his lap and then went into the kitchen. As she stood at the counter and waited for the coffee to brew, the sound of Tony talking and Joey's gurgling responses filled her heart.

She hadn't wanted to love the little boy, but it was impossible not to. She also hadn't wanted to care about Tony, but he was also weaving a path into her heart that would make it difficult to forget him when he was gone.

And eventually he would be gone. Even though Mick Blake had yet to find out anything about Amy's whereabouts, this current arrangement wouldn't last forever, nor should it. Sooner or later Tony would have to figure out what his future with Joey was going to look like.

With coffee cups in each hand, she returned to the living room and set the cups on the coffee table. Tony continued to hold Joey as they drank their coffee and talked about the craft fair.

"We travel to Dallas in the spring for a big craft fair there and then do this one in the fall," she explained.

"And doing those two fairs keeps you financially solid for the year?" he asked and then grimaced. "Not that it's any of my business."

"No, it's okay, and yes, between the two craft shows and my internet business, we do just fine." She looked at him curiously. "Have you ever thought about leaving the Holiday ranch and striking out on your own? Maybe working your own ranch?"

"Occasionally, the thought has crossed my mind, but I'm satisfied where I'm at. I enjoy the company of the other men and I don't have the burden of responsibility that comes with owning a place. We all just hope Cassie doesn't decide to sell the place."

"You think that might be possible?"

"Definitely. She's a New Yorker at heart and I know Raymond Humes has approached her a couple of times about buying the ranch."

"Raymond Humes and his men are a disgrace to this town," she replied.

He looked at her in surprise. "They've given you problems?"

"They say terrible things just beneath their breaths whenever I see them in town. They're a bunch of racist, unintelligent pigs." She flushed. "Sorry, just thinking about them gets me all riled up."

"All of us on the Holiday ranch feel the same way about them," he replied. "They've set fires on our property, taken down fences, and we even believe they've stolen cattle, but we can never find the evidence for Dillon to charge them with anything."

They continued to talk until nine, when Joey started fussing for his fill-up bottle before his bedtime. Mary fixed the bottle and then Tony fed Joey.

When Joey was finished with the bottle, Mary took him from Tony. "I'm just going to change him and then put him down for the night. I'll be right back."

She left the room and went into her bedroom to change Joey's diaper and put him in a pair of pajamas. When she was finished, she carried him into the spare room, where his playpen awaited him.

She placed him in the center of the pen and leaned down to stroke her finger down his baby cheek. "It's time to say good-night, little man," she said softly. "I hope your dreams are filled with sunshine and happiness."

When she straightened and turned around, Tony stood in the doorway and his dark eyes were lit with a fierce hunger that weakened her knees and stole her breath.

Heaven help her but she wanted him. She walked to where he stood and without saying a word he took her into his arms and she didn't protest.

As they kissed, she steered him down the hallway and into her bedroom. She was aware that this was wrong on a hundred different levels.

She knew she had to stay in complete control if this was going to happen. If she didn't maintain control, then things would spiral into an ugly mess.

She also knew no matter what she would regret it. But none of these thoughts could override her desperate desire for him.

"Mary, Mary," he murmured into her ear when the kiss ended. "I'm crazy with wanting you." His warm breath caused a shiver of pleasure to shoot up her spine.

His mouth found hers again in a hot and hungry kiss that nearly stole all of her breath away. He held her tightly enough against his body that she could feel he was already fully aroused.

As he kissed her, they moved closer to the bed. Although her mind was hazy with need, it wasn't so hazy that she didn't know what she needed to do in order to keep her most intimate secrets safe.

He moved his hands up and down her back and it was only when he began to stroke her bare skin beneath her T-shirt that she dropped to her knees in front of him.

"Mary." He groaned as she nimbly unfastened his belt and then his jeans. She pulled both his jeans and his boxers down to his knees and then stroked his hardness.

It would be easy to lose herself in the sensual haze that threatened to overtake her, but she couldn't. She had to remain completely in control.

When she took him into her mouth, he tangled his

hands into her hair and moaned with pleasure. The fire inside her only burned hotter.

She moved her lips up and down the velvet length of him and he grew harder with each of her movements. His harsh panting, coupled with her own quickened breathing, filled the room.

He grabbed her by the shoulders. "Mary, stop. I want to be inside you."

She stared up at him. "And I want the same thing." She got to her feet and then pulled off her underpants from beneath the skirt she wore and then lay back on the bed with the skirt bunched around her waist. "Quickly, Tony. I'm ready for you now."

He kicked off his boots and stepped out of his jeans and boxers. With his eyes half-glazed he crawled onto the bed between her opened thighs. He slid into her and at the same time took her lips with a ravaging hunger.

When the kiss ended, he stared intently into her eyes and began to stroke in and out of her. Mary reached up and pulled the tie that contained his hair at the nape of his neck.

Silky strands spilled around him, making him appear wild and beautiful as he took possession of her.

Sensations of pleasure raced through her as he moved faster and faster against her…into her. Her hands moved back and forth across his muscled back, loving the feel of his warm skin.

This was what she'd wanted, what she'd needed. She'd wanted his body against hers. She'd wanted his hot and hungry kisses. She felt so beautiful when he gazed at her.

He suddenly stiffened and moaned as he reached his climax. He leaned down and captured her lips once again, this time in a soft kiss that moved her more than anything.

He braced himself on his elbows and gazed down at her, a small frown line appearing across his forehead. "You didn't…"

"No, but it's okay."

He released a ragged breath. "This all happened so quickly. We didn't even use protection."

"There's nothing to worry about. I—I can't have children." She wanted up and away from him now. She'd been a fool to allow this…to encourage it in any way.

She gave his chest a shove. "I need to go to the bathroom."

He rolled off her and she jumped up and hurried into the adjoining bathroom, closing the door behind her.

"Stupid woman," she whispered to her reflection in the mirror. By making love with Tony, she'd probably set up the expectation in him that this was the beginning of something. But she knew it was both the beginning and the end. All she had to do was make sure before he left here tonight that he understood that.

When she left the bathroom, Tony was no longer in the bedroom. She pulled her panties back on and left the room. She found him seated on the sofa and the warm smile he gave her nearly stole her breath away. Yes, he would definitely expect things now that she couldn't give to him.

She sank down next to him and he immediately took her hand in his. She should jerk it away. She should tell him to take Joey and get out of her house, get out of her life. But she didn't. She allowed the warmth of his hand to surround hers, knowing that after tonight everything would change.

"Mary, you said you can't have children. What happened?" His somber expression and soft gaze invited her to share.

"When I was twenty-four, I was diagnosed with ovarian cancer. I had to have a complete hysterectomy to save my life." Thankfully, her voice didn't betray any of the tumultuous emotions that filled her when she thought of that terrible time in her life.

His hand tightened around hers. "I'm so sorry."

She shrugged and pulled her hand from his. "It was eight years ago and it feels like it happened in another life." She paused a moment and then continued, "Tony, about what just happened—"

"Next time we go slow," he interrupted, and his eyes once again filled with a hunger and a sweet promise. "Next time we take our time and I promise that you'll leave the bed completely fulfilled."

"Tony, there won't be a next time," Mary said and stood. "We just made a mistake and I'm not willing to make another one."

He looked at her in surprise. "Why was it a mistake? We're two adults who have an intense attraction to each other. We acted on that attraction tonight and there's nothing to stop us from acting on it again."

"I'm stopping it. Our relationship should remain social and not intimate, if nothing else but for the sake of Joey. Any continued intimacy will only complicate things between us. Besides, I'm just not interested in that kind of a relationship with you."

She hated the darkness that crept into his eyes, the frown on his lips and the lines of concern across his forehead.

"Okay, Mary. Of course I'll honor your wishes." He got up from the sofa. "And now I guess I should go."

"Yes, it's getting late and I'm tired." Relief shuddered through her as she walked him to the front door. It was done. She'd had him for a few minutes, and for those minutes had felt like a real woman, but now it was definitely done.

He turned to her and before she realized his intention he slowly trailed a finger down the side of her face, his gaze holding hers intently.

"Mary, whatever is between us is like a force of nature. I'm not sure either of us can control it." He dropped his hand back to his side.

"I can," she replied firmly. *She had to.* "We'll see you tomorrow night."

With a nod of agreement he left the house. She moved to the window, watched until his truck lights were swallowed by the dark of night and then went back into her bedroom.

A force of nature, yes, that was what had occurred tonight. It had been a hurricane that rained want, a tornado that had blown need and a volcano spewing white-hot flames of desire.

It could never happen again. Tonight she had controlled how things had unfolded between them. She had made sure that it was fast and frantic and without any foreplay, other than what she had done to him.

She couldn't take a chance that she'd be in control the next time and so there would never be a next time. There was no question that her feelings for Tony were growing, but she had to resist them…and him.

Stepping out of her skirt, she remembered how warm, how wonderful he'd felt against her. It had been so many years ago that she'd been in any man's arms. Tony's kisses had been magic and she would have loved to kiss him forever.

She tossed her skirt to the floor and then pulled off her T-shirt and threw it aside as well. A faint tremble began in her legs as she drew in a deep breath and squeezed her eyes tightly closed.

Turn around. Open your eyes and look at yourself, a little voice whispered in her head. *Remember how it was when you thought Rick loved you enough and then he turned away from you in revulsion.*

He swore he was in love with you, but he couldn't deal with the reality of your scars. Men don't want damaged goods.

Slowly she turned around to face the mirror she hadn't looked in for years. She still trembled when she opened her eyes and stared at the naked woman in the reflection.

Not a real woman, not with real breasts. They were the lumps that a plastic surgeon had put on her chest, lumps that were bisected with scars and without nipples.

They had no feeling, no sensations left for any kind of pleasure. They couldn't nurse a child. They were just useless lumps to fill out a blouse in an attempt to look normal.

Rick had told her he loved her, but the first time they were going to be intimate when he saw her naked, he just couldn't deal with it and he'd run. That had been two years ago and nothing had changed. Her body was still ugly enough that no man could ever love her.

She whirled around from her reflection as a sharp grief stabbed into her heart and squeezed her stomach. She grabbed her nightgown and yanked it on as tears burned hot at her eyes.

She turned off her bedroom light and crawled beneath the covers on her bed as the tears began to fall and she unleashed uncontrollable sobs.

Choctaw women were the givers of life. That was their place in the world, but Mary would never bear a child of her own. She would never have a husband or a family to love and support.

When she'd gotten ovarian cancer, she'd had no real choice. It was either have a hysterectomy or die and she'd chosen life. Because her mother and her mother's sister had both died of breast cancer, Mary had the genetic testing done. The test had come back with bad news. She had the BRCA gene mutation and as a result she faced another life-and-death decision.

Once again she had chosen life and had a double mastectomy and reconstructive surgery. It had been the safe thing to do. It had been the smart thing to do, all her doctors had assured her.

"You're a survivor," they'd told her.

The surgeon's work had made her appear normal

when clothed, but she wasn't normal. She was no longer a real woman.

Another sob racked her body and she turned her face into her pillow as a deep anguish tore through her.

She'd chosen life, but in doing so she'd demolished any chance she might have had for love. She'd effectively killed her heart and spirit—she'd destroyed her very soul. She was a survivor that nobody would want.

She was a healthy woman, but she was also a dead woman walking and nothing and nobody could change that.

Chapter 6

The morning of the craft fair dawned bright with sunshine and warm temperatures that would assure a nice crowd over the weekend.

Tony left the ranch at eight thirty on Friday morning to head for the old rodeo grounds on the west side of town, where the fair was to take place.

For the past two days he'd been unable to stop thinking about Mary and their lovemaking. It had been hot. It had been frantic and it had ended far too quickly.

Last night when he'd gone to her house after work she'd been a bit distant and closed off. Thankfully, Halena had sat in the living room with them and had filled in any silence that might have occurred with her lively chatter.

A rental truck was in the driveway and Halena had

explained that it had taken several hours during the day for the two of them to get everything loaded and ready to go. Tony tried to tell himself that Mary was probably just tired.

Still, he hated the possibility that their physical intimacy had ruined the emotional connection they'd been sharing. He'd enjoyed relaxing with her, sharing bits and pieces of his life and himself, and she had done the same.

Was he such a bad lover that he'd turned her off? He'd never had any complaints in that area before, but he'd also never left a woman unsatisfied before.

There just hadn't been time. She'd taken control of the situation and had brought him to near madness before he could rationally think. Hell, they hadn't even completely undressed. They'd acted like two horny teenagers groping each other in the backseat of a car.

Maybe it's because you just aren't good enough, a little voice whispered inside his head. *You'll never be worth anything. We're the only people who would have you. Nobody else wanted you.*

He squeezed his hands more tightly around the steering wheel and shoved the deep voice from his childhood away. Still, a bad taste lingered in his mouth.

He hoped his time with Mary at the craft fair would somehow take them back to the easy, comfortable relationship they'd shared before she'd taken him into her bedroom. And he couldn't help but hope that they would share that kind of physical intimacy again.

The old rodeo grounds had been abandoned for as

long as Tony could remember. The small town of Bitterroot wasn't on the circuit anymore.

However, the wide-open space was used when carnivals came to the area, or when the town council decided to put on a celebration of one kind or another. They even used it for the occasional concert when the powers that be managed to book a country-western star.

There was plenty of parking and lots of cars and trailers already there.

He expected the morning not to be too busy, but as the evening came there would be plenty of people. Tomorrow would be the big day. On a Saturday, when many folks didn't have to work, most of the townspeople would probably turn out for the fun.

In the distance multicolored tents rippled in the light breeze, along with more stable wooden structures. The scents of funnel cake, popcorn and other enticing food scents rode the air despite the morning hour.

The grounds were surrounded by an old wooden fence that had been built to keep people and kids from sneaking into an event they hadn't paid for, but the fence had never been high enough to keep determined cheaters from getting in.

Although Tony had never been to the annual craft fair before, he did know that it drew in people from all areas of Oklahoma and beyond to the small town of Bitterroot, not only as vendors but also as customers.

For the next three days the motel would be filled, the café would be busy and the local businesses would be crowded, making everyone happy.

He now got out of his truck and headed toward the

entrance gate. He looked forward to spending an entire day and evening with Mary and Joey.

He was pleased to see two of Dillon's men in uniform standing at the gate. Apparently, they were there to keep any rowdiness that might occur in check. "Good morning, Officer Ramirez, Officer Taylor," he greeted them.

"Tony, nice to see you," Ben Taylor returned. "Have you come out to buy something specific?"

"Or are you here to sample all the crazy food?" Juan Ramirez added with a pleasant grin. "Did you know they have deep-fried Twinkies?"

Tony laughed. "No, I didn't know that. Actually, I'm here to help out Mary Redwing and her grandmother," Tony replied.

"Halena pinched Juan's butt earlier," Ben said with a laugh.

A bit of red jumped into Juan's cheeks. "She said I had the sexiest butt she'd seen in years. I'm not planning on getting too close to their tent today."

Tony laughed and shook his head. Leave it to Halena to intimidate the police. He looked beyond the two officers. "Mary told me they have a light blue tent, but I see several in the distance."

Ben walked over and grabbed a piece of paper from a display board. "This shows the location of each business that's here for the weekend."

"Mary's tent is over there on the left," Juan said.

Ben looked down at the directions. "Aisle two, booth space six," he said and then handed Tony the paper.

"Thanks," Tony replied. He said goodbye and then

headed to the left. His heart stepped up its rhythm in anticipation of the day.

He'd been shocked when Mary had shared with him that she couldn't have children. He hated that she'd had to deal with cancer, but that certainly didn't change the way he felt about her.

And what did he really feel about her? He knew he liked her a lot and he also knew he was physically drawn to her. But he was surprised that when he left her at night he couldn't wait for the next evening to come when he'd see her again. He was surprised that she filled so many of his thoughts throughout the day.

And she didn't want that kind of a relationship with him…or did she? For the past couple of days she seemed to be sending him mixed signals.

His heart jumped as he caught sight of her. She stood in front of the large blue tent. Clad in a pair of tight jeans and a sky blue blouse, her hair hung in twin braids and a smile curved her lips as she saw his approach.

"Good morning," he said when he reached the tent.

"Same to you," she replied. "Welcome to our home away from home for the next three days." She gestured for him to step into the tent.

Halena sat in a chair at the back of the large space with Joey asleep in his bouncy chair at her feet and an electronic tablet in her lap. "Greetings, handsome warrior," she said with a smile.

"You look like a ray of sunshine," he replied. She wore a dazzling yellow skirt and matching blouse and both had intricate decorative beading.

"I'm a walking advertisement," she replied.

Tony looked around the space. Floor-to-ceiling plastic shelves held all shapes of baskets and pottery items, while dress racks held a variety of clothing. Fancy dream catchers hung from the ceiling along with wind chimes.

"Is all of this traditional?" he asked.

"Not all of it," Mary replied. "Some of it is just what people want from Native Americans. For instance, the dream catchers originally came from the Ojibwa people, not the Choctaw, but people love them and so Grandmother and I make them. They are one of our best sellers."

"They're gorgeous." He walked over to the pottery, awed by the beauty of each piece. One in particular captured his interest. It was a pale sand color and shaped like a pitcher. A silhouette of a Native American took center stage on the piece and he was framed by what appeared to be dark tear drops.

"There's a story to this?" he asked and pointed to the pitcher.

"The Trail of Tears," Mary said.

Tony frowned.

"Good heavens, don't tell me you don't know about the Trail of Tears," Halena exclaimed. "That historical event held our people's sorrow and showed our indomitable strength." She frowned at him. "What kind of a Choctaw are you that you don't know this?"

His stomach clenched as memories of his childhood suddenly assaulted him.

Indians don't sleep in the bed, they sleep on the floor. The deep male voice held nothing but contempt.

Tie him to the tree, he's nothing but a dirty injun. The sound of childish laughter filled his head as he remembered the bite of the tree bark at his back and the tight rope that held him in place.

"I was taught to hate that part of me." The words fell out of his mouth without volition.

Halena studied him for a long moment. "Then I must teach you to embrace the blood of our people that runs in your veins," she replied firmly.

At that moment Joey woke up and two buyers appeared in the tent. Relief fluttered through Tony at the interruption. As Halena stood to help Mary, Tony picked up Joey and held him close to his chest.

Joey deserved better than him as a father. How on earth could he teach Joey to be happy and proud when Tony had such self-loathing inside him?

The morning passed quickly with customers drifting in and out of the tent. While Mary greeted each person with a friendly smile, her thoughts were on the man who shared the tent space with them.

I was taught to hate that part of me. His words haunted her and created an unexpected pain inside her. They made her wonder more than ever what forces had driven him to be a runaway out on the streets. Who had taught him that hatred?

At noon he went to one of the food vendors and got them all big sandwiches and chips. In one of the lulls the man from the next tent stepped in to visit.

He was from Texas and sold cookbooks, cooking kits geared toward cowboys and old west fare. Tony bought one he said he was going to give to Cord Cully, aka Cookie, who fed all the cowboys at the Holiday ranch.

As the afternoon slipped away, business really began to pick up. Laughter rang in the air and people who stopped in the tent cooed and aahed over Joey and admired and bought a variety of items.

Joey was a little ham, grinning and laughing at each new face that appeared. She had tried to stay as detached from him as much as possible, but she had fallen completely and totally in love with the happy boy.

Her heart would break just a little bit when this arrangement with Tony ended, but she couldn't be his easy solution forever.

Eventually, if Amy never showed up again, Tony would have to figure out how to be a single parent on his own. In fact, Mary intended to talk to him in the next couple of days about ending her babysitting.

It had been almost two weeks since Amy had deposited the baby on Tony's doorstep and then disappeared, and with each day that passed Mary's belief that her friend would return soon waned. Sometimes Amy's drug benders went on for months before she'd once again make the attempt to get straight.

"Are you getting hungry?" Tony walked over to stand next to her.

Why did his very nearness race her heart? Throughout the day she'd been nearly overwhelmed by his presence. After making love with him, she'd been determined to distance herself from him.

However, it was so difficult to remain unmoved when he smiled at her, when his gaze was so soft the way it lingered on her. He made it difficult on her just by being.

"Mary?"

She startled as she realized she hadn't answered his question. "Yes, I'm getting hungry. Since you got lunch for us this afternoon, why don't I go get us some hot dogs for dinner."

"And funnel cake," Halena added.

"Are you sure you don't want me to get it?" he asked.

"No, in fact I'll take Joey with me. I could use a little fresh air and he can take the walk with me." She grabbed the baby backpack she'd bought when she and Halena had gone to the general store the day before.

She put it on and Tony grabbed Joey from his bouncy chair. "You want to take a little walk, Joey?" she asked.

He kicked his legs and grinned as if he understood every single word she'd said. Tony put him in the backpack and Mary left the tent.

She breathed in the evening air, which didn't smell of Tony's scent. Joey's light weight wasn't a burden and she hoped the little boy was looking at the bright colors of the tents and their surroundings. He wiggled around, obviously excited by whatever he saw.

The hot dog vendor was several aisles away and during the walk she was greeted by several familiar faces. Many of the vendors came back year after year, and although Mary didn't always remember all of their names, she knew them on sight.

She wove her way through the throng of people and finally reached the hot dog stand, where she stood in the line of hungry people looking for a quick dinner.

"Mary, it looks like you've been busy since last year," a familiar voice said.

Jed Baker stood next to her in line and pointed to Joey. Mary laughed. "Hi, Jed. He isn't mine. He belongs to a friend."

"He's a cute little fella."

"Thanks. How has business been today?" she asked. Jed came from Kansas and sold beautiful pieces of wood that he carved faces and figures into. He had explained to her that the wood spoke to him and told him whether it hid the face of a wolf or a fox or an old man.

"Not too bad. What about you?"

"It was a bit of a slow start, but sales have picked up this afternoon." They both took a step forward in the line.

"How's your grandmother?" Jed's eyes lit with amusement. "Is she still as ornery as ever?"

Mary laughed once again. "Definitely."

"Tell her I've got that special carving she asked me about for her whenever she can get away and come to my tent to get it. When we were here last year, she told me she wanted a carving of a naked man on horseback."

Mary groaned and rolled her eyes. "God bless that woman. I hope it isn't too obscene."

Jed laughed. "I tried to be as tasteful as possible."

"I'll tell her," she said and then it was her turn to order and they said goodbye.

Mary received her order and headed for the funnel cake vendor. Joey had apparently fallen asleep as he had stopped wiggling.

The crowd was growing bigger with every minute

and several times she was accidently jostled by children and teenagers who danced and raced around with the excitement of the fair.

She was almost to the funnel cake booth when she was jerked backward and Joey's weight shifted abruptly. In horror, she dropped the bag of hot dogs and whirled around.

A dark-haired man with an ugly snarl on his face stood inches in front of her. "Give Joey to me," he demanded.

"What?" She stared at him blankly. Surely she had misunderstood him.

He pulled a gun from his jacket pocket. "Give him to me now. He's mine."

Fear froze her in place. The crowd around them melted away as she stared into the man's dark and dangerous eyes. Her brain couldn't make sense of what was happening. Who was this man?

"Give him to me now," he repeated and raised the barrel of his gun to point at her chest.

In the space of her frantic heartbeat a million thoughts flew through her head. How did he know Joey's name? Why did he want Joey? What did he mean that Joey was his?

If he shot his gun right now, he'd risk the possibility of hurting the baby. If he shot her, he also risked immediate capture.

There were dozens of armed cowboys in the area, men who would instantly respond to a damsel in distress. With this thought in mind, she did the only thing she knew to do.

She screamed.

The scream pierced through the laughter and sliced through the happy conversations of the people nearby. "Help me! Somebody please help me, he's trying to take my baby from me," she cried.

"Hey, what's going on over there?" a deep voice called from somewhere on their left.

"What's wrong with you, man? Leave her alone," another man called out.

The dark-haired man took several steps back from her, slid his gun back into his pocket and then turned and ran, quickly disappearing into the crowd.

Mary released a sob at the same time Joey began to wail.

"Mary?" Tony appeared out of the crowd and raced toward her. "Mary, what happened? Are you all right?"

"I'm all right. Get Joey," she said and turned her back so he could get the crying baby out of the backpack. She turned back around and took Joey into her arms.

"What's going on?" Tony asked, his eyes narrowed as she hugged Joey close to her chest.

The people who had gathered around her began to drift away as Tony threw an arm around her shoulders. For a moment the fear of what had almost occurred made it impossible for her to speak.

"Call Dillon," she finally choked out. "A man just tried to kidnap Joey."

Tony gasped and pulled her closer against his side. "Let's get you back to the tent."

Neither of them spoke as they hurried toward the relative safety of the tent. Mary's thoughts continued to fly in a million different directions, each one more chilling than the last.

When they reached the tent, Halena took one look at them both and then jumped up from her chair. "What's happened?"

"A man tried to kidnap Joey." A shiver stole up Mary's spine. "He had a gun and he said that Joey was his." She hugged Joey tighter against her as she held Tony's gaze. "Amy told you to protect him from evil. I know in my soul I just met her evil."

Chapter 7

Tony stood at the front entrance of the tent with his hand on the butt of his gun. He'd called Dillon and as he awaited the arrival of the chief of police, his heart beat anxiously and his blood ran cold.

Ben Taylor stood on the outside of the back of the tent, on guard to make sure that nobody tried to come into the interior that way.

Joey was napping in Mary's arms and Halena sat next to Mary, her expression grim. For right now the business was closed and Tony kept any potential buyers and lookers out.

Who was the man who had accosted Mary? He'd obviously tried to use the crowd and the activity to his advantage. Thank God it hadn't worked.

He'd told Mary the baby was his and he'd known

Joey's name. *Oh, Amy, what kind of a web of lies have you put us in?* Tension tightened his stomach.

Had Amy told this man he was Joey's father? And if so, then what kind of a father pulled a gun and pointed it at a defenseless woman? What kind of a father tried to kidnap a baby?

His blood chilled even more as a new thought sprang into his head. Had the break-in that had occurred at Mary's house really been a thief trying to steal Native American items to sell, or had it been this man attempting to get to Joey?

What in the hell was going on and what drama had Amy cast them all into?

He released a small sigh of relief as he saw Dillon approaching with Officer Juan Ramirez. He had no idea what the lawman might be able to do, but he felt better already knowing that a report would be made.

"Tony." Dillon greeted him with a grim smile. He glanced into the interior of the tent and indicated for Tony to follow him inside. "Juan will keep people out while I speak to you all."

Tony nodded and followed Dillon to the back of the tent, where he greeted Mary and Halena with the same tight expression. He pulled a pad and pen from his pocket. "Tell me exactly what happened," he said to Mary.

Tony's blood chilled once again as she explained that she believed the man had first tried to grab Joey from the backpack. Thank God Joey had been buckled into the canvas seat. When she told Dillon that the man had then drawn a gun and demanded she give up the child, Dillon's features tightened even more.

"What did he look like?" he asked when she finished her story with the man disappearing into the crowd.

"He was maybe about six feet tall and had a slim build." She frowned and her lower lip began to tremble.

Tony fought the impulse to pull her up from the chair and take her into his arms, to somehow try to shield her from the fear that had entered her eyes.

"His hair was black and neatly cut and his eyes… His eyes were dark and wild-looking."

Once again Tony's stomach clenched with tension as she gave Dillon a description of the man's clothing. Tony was certain the man was no longer in the area. What worried him was that if what he was thinking was correct, then the man had made two attempts to steal Joey away.

"Maybe this evening after you close up here you could come down to the station and look at some mug shots," Dillon said as he tucked the pen and pad back into his pocket. "Who knows, maybe we'll get lucky and the man has a rap sheet."

Mary nodded. "We close up here at nine. Is that too late?"

Dillon smiled ruefully. "Not at all. Long nights have become a habit for me."

"If this man is really Joey's father, and it's obvious he knows Mary has Joey, then why didn't he just come to the front door to get his son?" Halena asked. "Why point a gun and try to kidnap him?"

Nobody had an answer for her. "One thing is for

certain," Tony said to Dillon. "There's no way I'm giving up Joey to any man who pulled a gun on Mary."

"I should have shot him the night when he tried to break in," Halena exclaimed. She looked at Dillon. "You know it had to have been him. I'm just giving you a heads-up—if he tries to break in again, I will shoot him through his black heart."

"We don't know for certain that he was the person who tried to break into your house," Dillon protested.

"I know," Halena replied. "The leaves on the trees have whispered to me and told me he's the heartless tin man I dreamed about. At first I thought the tin man was Tony, but now I see more clearly."

Tony had no idea what the old woman was talking about. All he knew for certain was that he had to step up and make sure that Joey, Mary and Halena remained safe until this whole mess was straightened out.

"I'll keep Juan here on guard for the rest of the evening," Dillon said as he walked with Tony toward the front of the tent.

"Thanks, I appreciate it," Tony replied. "But I don't intend to let Mary or the baby out of my sight until we get to the bottom of all this."

"You realize the odds of me finding this guy based solely on Mary's description of him is slim. We have a lot of dark-haired strangers wearing jeans and a jacket in town this weekend for the fair."

Tony frowned. "Whoever he is, he's got to be tied to Amy."

"And Mick hasn't been able to find out anything for you where she's concerned?"

"Nothing. It's like she disappeared into thin air." Tony couldn't help but worry about the woman he'd once shared a brief relationship with. Although he hadn't been in love with her, he had cared about her.

"It would help if Mary could pick this guy out of a mug-shot book," Dillon replied.

"I'll make sure she's there right after she closes down things here."

"Then I'll see you all later." With that Dillon turned and disappeared into the crowd.

Halena walked over to where Tony remained at the front of the tent. "I'll deal with the customers. You go sit with my granddaughter. I think she needs you more than me right now."

That was exactly where Tony wanted to be—next to Mary and the little boy who might or might not be his son. He was still horrified by what had happened and the expression of fear that lingered on Mary's features.

He sat in the chair next to her and gestured toward the sleeping Joey. "Why don't you let me take him for a little while," he said. "He must be getting heavy."

"He's fine." She released a shuddery sigh and gazed down at him. A smile curved Joey's lips, as if his dreams were happy ones. Thank goodness he was safe and sound.

"I'm sorry, Mary."

She looked at him in surprise. "Why are you sorry? You haven't done anything wrong."

"I brought danger to your doorstep."

"You didn't know this was going to happen," she replied.

"But now I know." He sighed. "Tonight after we go to the police station, I'll pack up Joey's things and take him back to the bunkhouse with me. It's the right thing to do. I can't have you and Halena in danger because of me and Joey."

"No, there has to be another way." She tightened her arms around the boy.

"I can't allow you to be involved in this any longer," he protested.

Her gaze held his steadily. "But I'm already involved. There has to be another way of handling this without suddenly uprooting Joey. We have him on a good routine. He's thriving right now."

Tony frowned thoughtfully. "The only other thing I can think of is if I take off work for a couple of weeks and move in with you and Halena."

Her eyes widened slightly and then she looked down at Joey. She swept a finger across one of his cherub cheeks and then gazed at Tony once again. "Then that's what we'll do. Three people guarding him is definitely better than one."

"Are you sure? We know now that there's a crazy man out there who wants him." He couldn't believe that she'd agreed to such a plan. If he was in her position, he would have run for the hills.

"I'm positive," she replied firmly. Her eyes shone with an inner strength and with complete commitment.

He stood. "Then I'll just call Cassie and make some arrangements. Maybe while you're in the station with Dillon I can run to the ranch and pick up a few things I'll need."

She nodded. "The most important thing is that we keep Joey safe from that man, no matter what it takes."

For the next couple of hours he worried about their decision. Was he doing the right thing, or was he putting two women he cared about at risk? Both of them understood there was risk and yet appeared determined to take it on.

The rest of the evening passed quickly and by the time they loaded up the merchandise into the truck for safe-keeping through the night, it was almost nine thirty.

They all got into Tony's truck and headed toward the police station on Main Street. It was a silent ride. Even Halena was quiet, as if the events of the day weighed heavily on her.

Tony had few illusions that Mary would be able to identify the man from any mug shots Dillon might have. If the man had been a Bitterroot native, then the odds were good that Mary would have known him when he'd attempted the kidnapping, but she hadn't known him.

Since Amy had moved to Oklahoma City, the man was probably from there as well. If that was the case, then it was doubtful that he'd ever gotten arrested in Bitterroot. Still, it was worth a shot.

Dillon greeted them in the small lobby area and took them into a conference room, where two large binders were on the long table. "Mary, while you go through those, I'm going to head to the ranch," Tony said. "I'll be back in less than an hour."

"It's going to take her at least that long to go through

all the photos," Dillon replied. "Since this afternoon I tried to update the mug shots from what I could get from Oklahoma City."

Mary settled in at a chair at the table with Halena seated across from her. She looked small and vulnerable as she began to look at the mug shots. Tony watched her for a moment and then he left the building.

Minutes later he was back in his truck and headed for the ranch. A tension headache pounded at the base of his skull. He'd called Cassie earlier and explained to her what was going on. She'd told him to take what time he needed, as he'd known she would. More than once since she'd taken over the ranch she'd stepped up to help people in need.

He was still surprised that Mary had agreed to this new arrangement and that she hadn't sent him and Joey packing immediately. He was nervous about what the future might bring, but he couldn't help the fact that having Mary and her grandmother on his side was oddly comforting.

He had no idea what to expect. How could he keep them all safe when he didn't know his enemy? How did he fight against an unknown entity? Somehow he had to make sure that he was on his guard for any hint of trouble.

If what he believed was right, then the man had already made two attempts to get Joey, and Tony had no question in his mind that a third attempt would happen sooner rather than later.

One thing was certain—danger was coming hard and fast.

* * *

Mary shifted positions on the hard chair and turned another page in the binder. Tony had returned and sat next to her while Halena sat across the table with Joey in her lap.

Dillon stood near the door. He'd been patient in the last hour while she'd gazed at face after face, seeking the man who had tried to attack her.

She was frustrated not only with the whole situation, but also with herself. She should have let them go, both Joey and Tony. He'd offered to take Joey and walk out of her life, but she'd protested.

There was no happy ending for her here. She was a fool to prolong the goodbyes that would inevitably occur. Joey wasn't her child and Tony wasn't her man. They were just passing ships that had brought her momentary happiness. And now there was another kind of danger.

But when push came to shove, she just wasn't ready to let them go. Besides, Joey wouldn't be as safe in day care as he was with her. With Tony in the house, she wasn't afraid. She knew he'd do everything in his power to keep them all safe. The decision they'd made was the best one for Joey and that brought her some comfort.

She frowned and focused once again on the photos. She'd been shocked by how many there were. She'd always considered Bitterroot a safe little town, but it apparently wasn't without criminals.

She flipped the page and suddenly froze. He stared up at her from the notebook, his eyes dark and evil and his thin lips twisted with a sneer.

"It's him." She stabbed her finger just below his neck. "This is the man." She fought against an inner shiver that threatened to overtake her.

Tony leaned closer and Dillon came around the table to stand behind her. "You're positive?" Dillon asked.

"One hundred percent." She looked up at Dillon. "Who is he?"

Dillon's gray eyes narrowed and his shoulders straightened. "He's bad news. His name is Ash Moreland. That mug shot is from a year ago when he was arrested in Oklahoma City on a petty drug charge that was eventually dismissed."

"Doesn't sound that bad to me," Tony replied.

"I'm not finished," Dillon replied. "Moreland is suspected to be a fairly powerful drug lord in Oklahoma City. He's also a prime suspect in three murders over the past year, but so far the authorities haven't been able to get enough evidence to make an arrest."

Mary's heart felt as if it stopped beating. A drug lord? A murderer? Dear God, what had Amy gotten involved in? What had she gotten *them* involved in? A deep chill shuddered through her as she gazed at the innocent little boy in Halena's arms.

"You're positive that's the man?" Dillon asked her.

She stared down at the photo in front of her and then looked up at him. "I'm a hundred-percent positive."

"Then I'll contact the Oklahoma City authorities and let them know what's going on here," Dillon continued. "If we get lucky, they might be able to arrest him at his home before the night is over."

"You'll keep us informed?" Tony asked.

"Absolutely," Dillon replied.

Mary stared down at the picture once again. *Protect him from evil.* That was what Amy had said to Tony. There was no question in Mary's mind that Ash Moreland was the evil Amy had feared.

Was it possible Ash was Tony's biological father? God help Joey if that was the case. And where was Amy? Was she someplace in hiding, or had Ash done something to her?

"There's nothing more to be done now," Tony said, pulling her from her terrible thoughts. "Let's get home."

Home…where Tony would now be staying. Some of her fear slowly ebbed away. He would make certain they all stayed safe. He would keep them all from evil.

They left the station with Dillon's promise that he would let them know what went down in Oklahoma City. It was only as they pulled into the driveway that Mary really processed the fact that for the next couple of weeks Tony would be with her every minute of every day.

This thought created a new kind of tension inside her. The last thing she wanted was for him to get any deeper into her heart.

He pulled his gun when they got out of the car and he hurried them inside. "Wait here," he said as they stepped just inside the front door.

He disappeared into the kitchen and then headed down the hallway. When he returned, the grim set of his lips had relaxed. "Okay, there's nobody here. I'm just going to get my things from the truck."

As he disappeared back outside, Halena moved into

the living room and sat on the sofa with Joey's car seat at her feet. The baby slept peacefully, unaware of the drama that swirled around him.

"He's a good man, Mary," Halena said. "He looks at you with both tenderness and desire. You could do far worse."

"That's not the tune you were humming about him a week ago," Mary replied.

"Things are clearer now in my head."

"It doesn't matter. This isn't about me and Tony," Mary scoffed. "This is about that baby and keeping him safe from that man and that's all there is to it."

Halena gave her a sly smile. "I see the way you look at Tony. You care about him."

A warm flush swept into Mary's cheeks. "Enough, Grandmother. You know I'm damaged goods."

Halena's smile vanished. "You are only damaged in your own mind, Granddaughter, and you can change the way you think about yourself."

At that moment Tony came into the house with a duffel bag. He dropped it on the floor and gazed at them both, obviously sensing the tension that crackled in the air. "Everything okay?"

"Everything is fine," Mary replied and shot a warning look at Halena. The conversation they'd shared was a familiar one, a conversation that set Mary's teeth on edge.

As if there wasn't enough going on, the last thing she needed at this moment was for her grandmother to lecture her about her body image. Her grandmother hadn't had her breasts cut off. She couldn't put herself in Mary's shoes.

"I'm going to work on a blog about shielded hearts and foolish women," Halena said and stood. "You don't have to worry about anyone coming in through my bedroom window. I'll sleep with my shotgun and I'll shoot first and ask questions later."

"I'll bunk here." Tony pointed to the sofa.

"Perfect," Mary said briskly. "I'll just go get some bedding for you." She walked down the hall to the linen closet. Had he thought she would invite him to sleep in her bed? No way, no how.

While the idea of falling asleep in Tony's strong arms was heavenly, there was no way she would allow any opportunity for intimacy to happen. They were simply two people trying to keep a baby safe and nothing more.

"You're welcome to put your toiletries in the hall bathroom," she said when she returned to the living room with two sheets and a blanket for him. "And you can also use the closet in the spare bedroom for any clothes you need to hang. I'm just going to go ahead and get Joey into his bed."

She bent down and picked up Joey, conscious of Tony's gaze lingering on her. "I'll be back in a few minutes."

Tenderness and desire.

Wasn't that what any woman would want to see in a man's eyes? She shook her head to dispel her grandmother's words.

She didn't bother putting Joey into pajamas. Instead she changed his diaper and then placed him in the playpen and covered him with a blanket. He didn't even wake up.

She remained standing over him for several long moments, breathing in his sweet baby scent and smiling as he blew a little spit bubble in his sleep.

Her heart already ached with his absence despite the fact that he was still with her. She had to prepare herself to say goodbye to Joey, but hopefully not until any danger to him had passed.

When she returned to the living room, Tony had made out his bed on the couch and now stood in front of the window and stared outside.

His back was so broad and his hips so lean, and the ponytail that fell down beneath his shoulders looked rich and soft.

He turned to face her and without saying a word he walked over to her and pulled her into his arms. She stiffened against him.

"Just let me hold you for a minute, Mary," he whispered softly into her ear. "I don't want anything else from you right now, but I've wanted… I've needed to do this since the moment I saw you with such terror in your eyes."

As the memory of Ash Moreland and his gun filled her head, she slowly relaxed into Tony's embrace. She wrapped her arms around him and leaned her head into the crook of his neck. She savored his familiar scent, a scent that made her feel safe for the first time since she'd looked into Ash Moreland's eyes.

"I was so afraid," she admitted. "I've never been so terrified in my life. I didn't know what he was going to do. I was so afraid he was going to shoot me and steal Joey away."

"I won't let him get close to you again." There was a firm conviction in his voice. "I won't let him get close to you or Joey."

She felt the kiss he wanted to give her. She knew with a woman's instinct that when she raised her head he would be ready to take her lips with his.

She couldn't allow it. She wanted him so badly, but she had to deny herself, she had to deny him. Abruptly she dropped her arms to her sides and stepped back from him so fast there was no time for a kiss.

"It's been a long day. I need to get some sleep. We all need to be up early in the morning to go back to the craft fair. Good night, Tony."

She practically ran from the living room and into her bedroom. She told herself that her pounding heart was due to the attempted kidnapping that afternoon and not because of being in Tony's arms.

She undressed in the dark and grabbed her nightgown from a drawer. Hopefully when she awakened in the morning Tony would have heard from Dillon that Ash was in jail. The danger would be over and everyone could get on with their lives.

A drug lord and a murderer. If the suspicions about Ash Moreland were true, then he probably wouldn't hesitate to kill to get what he wanted.

She pulled her nightgown on and then walked over to her window and peered outside. Bright moonlight spilled down on the back lawn and painted it with silvery illumination. In the distance the trees were black silhouettes against the starry night sky.

The night was still, as if the wind held its breath in

anticipation of something happening. Someplace out there was a man who scared her. Was he out there now? Watching the house and just waiting for another opportunity to get to Joey?

She left the window and got into bed. She closed her eyes and thought about being held in Tony's arms. He'd said he needed to hold her and she admitted to herself that she'd needed to be held by him. She released a deep sigh.

Outside was a man who wouldn't hesitate to kill her to get Joey, and inside was a man who was slowly killing her with sweet promises of what could never be.

Ash cursed when he saw the police presence at his house. He was almost a block away and decided to turn his car around and drive in the opposite direction.

Somehow he'd apparently been identified. They had to be at his house because of the botched attempt to get his kid back at the fair. Dammit.

He'd done his homework and had asked around about Mary. When he'd learned that she would be at the fair, he'd chosen not to make another attempt at her house. He'd decided to be patient, thinking that the fair would be the perfect opportunity to get Joey back.

He should have killed the bitch and grabbed the kid. Instead he'd choked, afraid that if he did what he wanted he'd earn himself a bullet in the back from some do-gooder cowboy.

Okay, so he couldn't go home. Not a problem. Ash had plenty of places where he could hole up. He had people who feared him, people who would take him in, feed him, give him their vehicle to use and not turn him in to the authorities.

If Mary Redwing and her cowboy lover thought they could keep Joey away from him, then they were fools. And fools deserved to die.

Chapter 8

"I appreciate your help," Tony said to Sawyer the next morning.

"No problem," Sawyer replied. "I'd much rather act as a bodyguard today instead of mucking out horse stalls or shining up saddles."

The two men stood just outside the tent where Halena and Mary were ready for another day of business. Tony had called Sawyer to come and spend the day with them as additional backup. He wasn't taking any chances with their safety.

"Clay said he'll be here after work to hang out with us," Sawyer added. "And Brody and Mac said all you need to do is call them if you need more men."

The bond Tony had with his fellow cowboys filled his chest with a burst of warmth. "I just know we're going to have a big crowd today and I want somebody armed to be with Joey all the time."

"Not a problem, brother." Sawyer clapped him on the back. "We've got it covered. It's just too bad the police couldn't get this bad actor in handcuffs last night."

"According to Dillon the police sat on Ash's house all night long and he never showed up. They have no idea where he might be. He must have somehow gotten a heads-up that the police were looking for him." Tony glanced into the tent, where Mary was straightening a rack of clothing and Halena held Joey.

He'd had a restless night on the sofa. As if his concern for them wasn't enough, the entire house smelled of Mary's fragrance, and the knowledge that she was only a few steps away in the bed where they'd made love had kept him tossing and turning all night.

The morning had been a bit frantic as they'd eaten a quick breakfast and headed to the fair, where they'd unloaded the truck and set up the sale items again.

Tony had been on guard. He now knew what the enemy looked like and there was no way Ash Moreland would get anywhere near any of them.

Within minutes the fair would be officially open once again and the exceptionally nice weather on a Saturday assured that plenty of people would be attending.

Would Ash come back today? Would he try to make another attempt? The crowd would be thick with people. Would he try to hide his dark hair beneath a hat? Attempt to sneak into the tent with a group of others? Tony had to be ready for anything.

Mary appeared ready to face the day. She was stunning in a pair of black jeans and a red T-shirt with black beading around the neckline. Once again her hair was in long twin braids that fell forward over her breasts.

She finished straightening the clothing and then moved over to the basket display and made final adjustments there. Her gaze caught his and she offered him a small smile that shot straight to his heart.

He'd sensed her strength in the few hours he'd spent with her when he'd come to her home to visit with Amy. But in the last twenty-four hours, he'd seen an inner core of strength in her that awed him.

She could have easily surrendered Joey to an armed man the day before. Instead she had risked her own life by refusing to comply with his command and had instead taken a risk and had screamed.

She also could have told him to take his son and go. He'd even offered to do that, but she'd insisted that together they would be better at protecting Joey. Together... he liked the way that sounded.

"I'll hang out here at the tent entrance," Sawyer said, bringing Tony back to the here and now. He leaned closer to Tony. "Just try to keep Mary's grandmother away from me. She's pinched my butt twice since I got here."

Tony couldn't help the smile that stretched his lips. Halena and her often outrageous actions and words definitely kept things interesting.

"I'll do my best to protect you from the big, bad grandma," he replied. "You just keep an eye out for Ash Moreland."

"You can count on me," Sawyer replied.

The Holiday cowboys had always counted on each other, and that was why Tony would never believe that one of them had committed the murders that had taken place so long ago.

Just as he had expected, the morning was busy and sales were brisk. Sawyer remained next to the entrance. He gazed at each man that approached with narrowed eyes and his hand on the butt of his gun.

As Mary and Halena took care of customers, Tony sat in the back of the tent with Joey. The little boy was sleeping less and interacting more with everyone with each day that passed.

At noon, Sawyer went for their lunch of the hot dogs and funnel cake they hadn't eaten the night before while Tony stayed on guard.

"Funnel cake is a gift from the gods," Halena said as she ate the last of the sweet treat.

"Personally I'm fond of apple pie," Tony replied.

"I like my apples in cider with a nice kick of booze," Halena replied.

"Speaking of cider, Cassie is planning a barn dance sometime around Halloween," Tony said. "You and Mary will have to come." He smiled inwardly as he thought about holding Mary in his arms as the Croakin' Frogs band played a slow song.

"I don't believe you're thinking of apples anymore, Tony Nakni, not with that loony smile on your lips," Halena observed.

Tony laughed. "I'm going to go spell Sawyer at the front. He's been standing for quite a while and could probably use a little sit-down time."

"You can send that hunky man right back here to me," Halena replied with a twinkle in her eyes.

It was just after they'd eaten that Dillon stopped by the tent. He greeted them pleasantly, but with the bad news that Ash still wasn't under arrest.

"He's apparently gone underground," Dillon said. "And his network is big enough that there isn't enough police manpower to try to hunt him down."

"And so we just wait for him to make another move," Tony said grimly. "And you know he will make another move."

Dillon gazed at Sawyer, and at Clay, who had arrived minutes before Dillon. He then looked back at Tony. "Looks like you've called in the troops."

"Just a little extra security while we're out here in public," Tony replied.

"And still no word from Amy?"

Tony shook his head, the fear he hadn't spoken aloud now rising up inside him. "I think she might be dead, Dillon. It's been almost two weeks ago that she dropped Joey off with me and nobody has seen or heard from her since that night."

Dillon sighed. "I'll check with all the hospitals in the area and the morgue in Oklahoma City, but two weeks isn't that long for a woman to be gone, especially one who might be doing drugs."

"I hope I'm wrong," Tony replied. "I hope she is just holed up someplace and will quickly get her act together and get back here."

Dillon's radio crackled and he grabbed it from his belt. He stepped back from Tony and listened to the voice at the other end. "I've got to go," he said to Tony. "Apparently, there's some sort of a fight going on near one of the booths."

Tony watched Dillon leave and his head was still filled with thoughts of Amy and what might have happened to her. Had she been running from Ash? Was that the trouble she'd been in? And if so, had the man found her and killed her? Or was it possible she'd holed up in some seedy motel room and OD'd?

No, he didn't want to think such dark thoughts. She might have run from Ash, but she was probably at a friend's place or in some motel partying.

"Everything okay?" Mary asked, a line of worry creasing her forehead as she stepped up next to him.

Tony looked into the tent, where Halena was helping a customer and Clay held Joey on his lap. "As okay as it can be," he replied. "Why do you ask?"

"When you were speaking to Dillon, you got such a troubled look on your face. I know you were thinking bad thoughts."

He smiled at her. "Have we gotten so close that you can now read my mind?" How he wished he could read hers. She was still more than a bit of a mystery to him.

She returned his smile. "I can't read your mind, but I can read some of your expressions." Her smile faded. "So, what were you two talking about?"

"Amy." He hesitated a moment, unsure if he should share with her what he'd been worried about. *She can handle it*, he thought. She'd probably been worried about the same things he had been. "Dillon is going to check with all the hospitals to see if she's a patient in one of them. He's also going to check with the morgue in Oklahoma City."

Mary's eyes darkened in sorrow and she slowly nodded. "I always believed Amy's life here on earth would be short. Still, I hope she's alive somewhere. Are you still in love with her?"

Tony took a step backward in surprise. "Why would you ask that?"

She averted her gaze from his and stared at some point over his shoulder. "It would be good for Joey if you and Amy would somehow find your way back to each other and build a life together."

"Mary, that's never going to happen. I'll admit I was infatuated with her for a while, but I was never in love with her." He might have believed he still had a little love in his heart for Amy if he hadn't gotten so close to Mary.

The feelings he had for the woman standing next to him were far deeper, far more profound than anything he had ever felt for Amy. He was convinced it wasn't love, but he wasn't sure exactly what it was. It was something he'd never experienced before with any woman.

As several more people entered the tent, Mary drifted away to attend to them. The rest of the afternoon flew by and at dinnertime Clay got them all barbecue sandwiches and chips from one of the food vendors.

Tony's nerves had been in knots all day and it was only as the end of the night drew near that he began to relax a bit. Tomorrow the craft fair would be open only until noon.

He'd be glad when they were all spending the days and nights in the safety of Mary's house and not out in a crowd, where it was difficult to see danger approaching.

His stomach clenched once again. He didn't want to think about the future, about what he'd do when the two-week vacation he'd taken from work was over and he still had no answers as to Amy's whereabouts.

Don't look to the future and never look back, just live in the moment. That had always been his mantra, but it was difficult to live that way now with a little boy and two women depending on him to keep them safe and a madman who wanted to destroy what little piece of happiness Tony had managed to find.

"That's the last of it," Mary said Sunday afternoon as she took the last piece of pottery out of the rental truck and handed it to Halena to carry into the garage, where shelving awaited the last of what hadn't sold over the weekend.

"Thank goodness we almost sold out of everything," Halena said. "This old woman is too tired to carry in another thing. Let's get inside, where I can put on some comfy clothes and get my feet up."

"Sounds good to me," Mary replied. She smiled at Tony, who held Joey in his arms. "Now it's back to normal life."

"We don't have normal in our life," Halena exclaimed.

Mary took Joey from Tony's arms as they approached the front door. As usual, Tony ushered them just inside the door and then he checked the rest of the house before allowing them to go any farther.

"It's clear," he said when he returned to the front door. He holstered his gun and Mary released a small sigh of relief. It was hard for her to believe that her life now included a man with a gun who searched the house for a bad guy each time they entered the premises.

Still, as Joey snuggled closer to her, she knew it was a small inconvenience to keep him safe. "I love working the craft fairs, but it's always a relief when it's over," she said.

She placed Joey in his bouncy seat and then gazed at Tony. "Are you hungry? Breakfast seems like it was a long time ago."

"I could eat," he replied.

"I've got some ham and cheese for sandwiches." She scurried into the kitchen and realized she was a bit nervous with the realization that Tony was going to be in the house day and night.

The last two nights hadn't been so difficult and with the craft fair there had been so much activity and other people around. But now it was just the four of them and she certainly wasn't accustomed to having a handsome man who she'd made quick, wild love with underfoot for twenty-four hours a day.

He joined her in the kitchen and as he helped her get the cold cuts out of the refrigerator their shoulders bumped. A current of electricity shot through her at the simple casual contact.

Jeez, what was wrong with her? She admitted that she was attracted to Tony, but she also recognized that he was forbidden fruit.

The last thing she wanted was to part from Tony

with the memory of revulsion in his eyes. Right now she held tight to the hunger, the fire that had sparked from his eyes when they'd made love. That was what she wanted to remember forever.

As she sliced a tomato, Tony washed off lettuce leaves, and by the time they had everything on the table Halena reappeared. She'd changed from her beautiful Native American dress to a pair of zebra-print sleep pants and a neon-green T-shirt with a howling coyote on the front.

Joey slept as the three of them sat at the table and ate their sandwiches. Their conversation revolved around the weekend activities and all the people they had seen.

"Tony, when we finish eating, would you help me hang my naked man in my room?" Halena asked.

The naked man on horseback carved into a piece of wood had been a big hit with Halena. Mary was only grateful Halena hadn't insisted they hang the darned thing in the living room.

"No problem," Tony replied easily.

Everything was so easy with him. Conversation flowed without strain. He'd handled everything that had happened with aplomb. He made her feel safe without effort and her grandmother had embraced him into their life as if he belonged with them.

And he didn't belong.

She had to remember that when she awakened in the morning and smelled the scent of shaving cream and his familiar cologne. She needed to remind herself that he didn't belong here when he filled the room with his laughter, when his dark eyes gazed at her with such an inviting heat. He made her feel beautiful and that made him oh, so dangerous.

She was relieved when after the meal he followed Halena down the hallway to her bedroom. They'd been back at the house for only about an hour and already his presence had her off center.

After cleaning up the kitchen, she went into the living room, where Joey had awakened and greeted her with a wide grin. "Hey, little man," she said and bent down to pick him up.

With one hand she held him and with the other hand she dropped the blanket on the floor so he could roll around and play. With the baby situated she sank down on the sofa.

There was no question that she was tired. Maybe that was why her mind was going so many crazy places. She hadn't slept well for the past two nights with the memory of that moment with Ash Moreland and his gun. That fact, combined with the adrenaline of working the fair and being around Tony, had left her exhausted.

Tony's deep laughter rang out from Halena's bedroom, and the pleasant sound twisted a knife into her heart. She reminded herself that even if she was a whole woman, that didn't mean Tony would even want to belong here forever.

He'd told her he didn't want to marry, but he'd also made it clear that he wanted her. Even if she took a chance with him, there was no reason to believe he'd stick around.

She smiled at Joey, who cooed and gurgled as he played with his fingers. Tony had also said he didn't want to be a father, and yet over the past two weeks he'd definitely grown into the position.

He might profess that he didn't love Joey, but his love for the child was in his every touch, in the way he gazed at the boy. He held Joey with such tenderness, and when he spoke to him, his voice held a wealth of love.

Whether he knew it or not, Tony had already embraced the role of father. And she couldn't help believing that someday with the right woman, he might realize he desired to be a husband, too. He might possibly want to have more children and build himself a real family.

Tony and Halena returned to the living room. "He hung it on the wall across from my bed, where I can look at the naked warrior every morning and every night," Halena said with satisfaction as she sat in the chair across from the sofa.

Mary's breath hitched in her chest as Tony sat next to her. "Hey, little buddy." He leaned forward and grinned at Joey, who laughed and waved his fists.

"I've never seen such a good baby," Halena said.

Tony leaned back. "Mary wasn't a good baby?"

"She was terrible," Halena replied with an affectionate look at Mary. "She came into this world wailing like a banshee and she continued to wail for about the next three months. Her mother was beside herself, certain that she was doing something wrong, but no matter how often Mary was fed and changed and rocked, she cried. And then one day she just stopped and I don't think she's cried since then."

Oh, Mary had definitely cried since then. She'd cried when she'd had her hysterectomy. She'd sobbed when she'd had her double mastectomy. She'd wept bitter tears when Rick had walked away from her. And she'd cried knowing that she and Tony would never share any more intimacy.

But she always cried alone, in her room…in the dark where nobody could see or hear her. She didn't want anyone to know the depth of her self-loathing—she needed to appear strong for those around her. Dammit, she *was* strong, she told herself.

Tony looked at her in amusement. "So, basically your grandmother is saying that you were a real crybaby."

Mary laughed. "Maybe it was because the leaves on the trees whispered in my ear that the day would come when my grandmother would move in with me."

"Ha, you're not that funny," Halena retorted, making both Tony and Mary laugh again.

The afternoon passed pleasantly with them talking about all the people they had seen at the fair, how successful the event had been for Mary's business and how nice Clay and Sawyer had been to show up and help out. They had all taken turns playing and interacting with Joey in between his feeding and naps.

They steered clear of any mention of kidnapping and Ash Moreland, which was fine with Mary. She didn't want to think about the horrible man who wanted possession of sweet Joey.

Dinner was eaten and at eight thirty Mary put Joey down for the night and Halena disappeared into her bedroom. Despite Mary's tiredness, she was too wound up to sleep so early.

"Do you want me to go into my bedroom so you can make out your bed?" she asked Tony.

"Nah, I'm not ready for sleep yet. Why don't we just sit and relax for a while longer." He took his gun out of the holster on his belt and placed it on the coffee table next to where he sat on the sofa.

She sat next to him and relaxed into the corner of the cushions. "You look tired," he observed.

"I am tired," she admitted. "It was a long weekend."

"Now that the fair is over, what do your normal days look like?" he asked.

"We get to work for the spring fair. I start weaving baskets and making pottery and Grandmother begins to sew. We have a daily routine that's fairly laid-back."

"I don't want you to change anything with me here. The last thing I want to be is a distraction."

He couldn't help that he was a distraction. His very presence changed the weight of the air, his energy exuded from him, and no matter where she was in the house, she felt him.

"We'll get through this," she replied. *I was taught to hate that part of me.* The words he'd said during the fair suddenly popped into her mind and with it came a hundred different questions.

"Of course we will," he replied. "We have to in order to save Joey." His dark eyes filled with a steely determination. "No matter what happens, Joey has to have a wonderful childhood and I know for certain he'll never have that with Ash Moreland."

She knew she shouldn't ask, she knew she shouldn't care, but that didn't stop her. "You want Joey to have the childhood that you didn't have." She leaned toward him. "Tell me, Tony. Tell me what happened to you. Tell me what drove you to the streets when you were so young."

For a long moment she thought she'd overstepped her place as myriad emotions swept over his face. Pain, sorrow and a soft vulnerability were quickly usurped by an expression of anger and she was suddenly sorry she'd asked. She was afraid to hear his story.

She was afraid it might break her heart.

Chapter 9

Tony's chest tightened as dark and painful memories filled his head. He never talked about his past with anyone. He stared at Mary and for the first time in his life he wanted to give that inner pain a voice.

"I was raised by Betty and Hank Ryan. They lived on a small ranch just outside of Oklahoma City and had three children of their own. I was told by them that my mother, a full-blooded Choctaw, gave me to them when I was nine months old."

"Why did she give you away?"

"They told me that my father was a drunk who'd left her and she didn't want me anymore. I don't know why the Ryans took me in. They didn't officially foster me, so they weren't getting any money, and they never adopted me. I think my mother must have given them some money or something up front. I never could figure out why they took me in."

He paused, dark emotions once again pressing against his chest. He had never wanted to share this with anyone, but for some reason Mary felt safe. Her soft gaze encouraged him to let it all out. He knew instinctively she wouldn't judge him in any way.

"I was the dirty Indian in their home," he continued. "I slept on the floor and ate their scraps. The only time I was allowed to clean up and dress in good clothes was when we all went to town for something or on the few days off and on when I was allowed to attend school. They worked me like a mule around the ranch, and when I wasn't working, their kids took great pleasure in tying me to trees or throwing me in the pigpen."

Now that the words had begun he couldn't stop them. "I was told daily that I had no place in the world, that the Choctaw nation didn't want me and that all white people would shun me." He paused to take a deep breath.

"Oh, Tony." Mary scooted closer to him and took his hand in hers. He welcomed the warmth of her hand as an icy chill had gripped his heart the moment he'd gone backward in time.

He couldn't begin to describe a young boy's confusion about the way he was treated. He couldn't find the words to explain how hungry he had been to belong.

"I tried so hard," he finally said. "I worked hard in an effort to make Hank happy. I tried to do whatever he wanted me to do. I picked flowers and made little things to give to Betty in hopes that she would give me a hug or tell me she loved me."

A bitter laugh escaped him and Mary squeezed his hand tighter. He stared at the wall over her shoulder. "There were no hugs for the Indian boy, no kind words at the end of a long workday. There was nothing but ridicule and scorn." Lost…he was lost in the miasma of pain and despair.

He smelled the disgusting odor of the pigs in the air, felt the sharp bite of a belt across his back and tasted the mishmash of slop that he was fed each day. His bedroom had been a thin mattress on the floor on the back porch. He'd frozen in the winter months and sweltered in the summer.

He'd been a thing, not a person. He'd been a possession to be used and abused. He'd grown to hate them, but he hated himself more. If he hadn't been a halfbreed, maybe they might have loved him. If he didn't have Native American blood running in his veins, maybe he would have really been part of the family.

"And so eventually you ran away." Mary's soft voice pulled him out of the darkness.

He gazed at her once again. "I was fourteen years old, almost fifteen, and on that particular night Hank had beat me with a belt because I'd asked for a second piece of bread at dinner. I was so angry, and I knew that night that if I stayed I'd probably wind up killing Hank or their oldest son, who was a constant torment to me."

He looked deep into her eyes but saw no judgment, no hint of revulsion in the soft depths. Her hand remained clasped warmly around his…an anchor to keep him from getting completely lost in his wretched past.

"I had no plan and I took nothing with me except the

clothes on my back. I left the Ryan ranch at midnight and headed for the streets of Oklahoma City."

"You must have been so frightened."

"I was," he admitted. "But I was more afraid to stay."

"What did you do?"

"Thankfully, it was summertime and I didn't have to worry about harsh winter weather. I found a place under an overpass to stay, and when I got hungry, I stole whatever I could from nearby stores. It's not something I'm proud of, but I was in survival mode and nothing else mattered."

"Did you have a plan for your future?" She searched his face as if wanting to know all of his secrets.

A small laugh escaped him. "When you're out on the streets, you don't think about your future. I didn't believe I had a future. All I thought about was when I'd be able to eat again and if I could get through the day without getting beat up."

"Who was beating you up on the streets?"

"There was a gang of skinheads who beat up anyone who wasn't white. I usually managed to get away from them, but occasionally they caught me and beat the snot out of me."

He offered her a small smile. "It's funny, I could take the beatings from them far better than the ones from Hank."

Her eyes darkened. "That's because Hank was the man who raised you, the man who should have protected and loved you. So, how did you get to be here in Bitterroot and on the Holiday ranch?" She released his hand and leaned back once again.

"That was the doing of a very special social worker named Francine Rogers." Tony smiled as he remembered Francine's cocoa-colored features and her gentle smile.

"She often hit the streets in the late evenings looking for runaways. She'd sometimes have food or blankets and she always wanted to help. She tried to help some of the boys reunite with their parents and get some of them into shelters. I'd talked to her several times before. She knew I was never going back to Hank and Betty and she also knew I wasn't interested in living in a shelter. One night she asked me if I'd like to go to Bitterroot and work on a ranch for a woman who was alone and needed help. I figured I had nothing to lose, so she took me to Cass Holiday."

The tension that had twisted Tony's guts slowly eased. "I found a home with Cass and the other men. There I'm not half-Choctaw or half-white, I'm just another cowboy."

"You're so much more than that, Tony," she replied. "You're an honorable man and you're smart and have a great sense of humor."

"Thanks." He searched her beautiful features. "I can't believe I told you about my childhood. I've never told anyone about my past before. You're good for me, Mary. You're like no woman I've ever known before."

Her gaze held his for a long moment and he wondered if she saw his desire for her in his eyes. "I'm glad you told me, Tony. And on that note, I think it's time for me to go to bed."

He watched with a small twinge of disappointment

as she got up from the sofa. He'd obviously made her uncomfortable and that was the last thing he'd intended.

He got up as well and walked with her down the hall. His bedding was folded up in the linen closet. "Mary?" He touched her arm just before she was about to turn to go into her bedroom.

She turned to look at him. "Are we okay?" he asked worriedly.

"We're fine, Tony." She released a small sigh. "My heart is just broken for a little boy who was so badly abused. I ache for that child who wanted to be loved, the boy who grew into a man who is now afraid to love."

He shook his head and the tension once again swelled in his chest. "It's not that I'm afraid to love, it's just that I choose not to love."

"And so Hank and Betty win. They managed to completely destroy you. Good night, Tony."

Before he could reply she stepped into her room and closed the door behind her. Tony stared at the door for several long moments before he finally turned to get his bedding.

Her words rang in his ears as he made his bed on the sofa. They echoed in his brain as he stripped down to his boxers, turned off the light and then slid in beneath the sheet.

He thought about the baby who may or may not be his. The child's laughter delighted him. The way he curled his little fingers around Tony's thumb shot a wave of protectiveness through him. Each and every expression enchanted him.

Did he love Joey? He could put no other name on the

emotions Joey evoked in him. He couldn't deny it. He loved Joey and he never wanted the boy to know the kind of fear and misery Tony had experienced when growing up.

As he stared up at the dark ceiling and waited for sleep to overtake him, his thoughts once again went to Mary. He loved the way she smiled. He loved how he felt when he was in her presence. Already he looked forward to seeing her in the morning and spending the day with her and Joey.

His desire for her was off the charts. One intimate encounter with her wasn't enough…would never be enough for him. Was he in love with her?

His heart beat a little faster. Whatever he felt for Mary scared him. She had made it clear she didn't want a relationship with him and the last thing he wanted was to be vulnerable enough with her that she'd have any opportunity to break his heart.

And yet as his eyes drifted closed, the leaves of the trees whispered softly in his ear that it was already too late to shield his heart.

He was falling in love with Mary.

Mary awakened before six. Dawn light wasn't even a promise on the horizon yet. Joey normally didn't wake up until seven or seven thirty and so there was no reason for her to jump out of bed and begin the day.

She rolled over on her back and thought about the night before and everything she'd learned about Tony's past. It had been tragic on so many levels.

He'd been taught to hate his Native American blood

before he could ever learn to be proud. And that was only one of the sins of his "parents." Beaten and half-starved, ridiculed and unloved, it was a wonder he was as well-adjusted as he was today.

That was probably due to Cass Holiday. If Tony's background was typical of the other men who'd come to work for Cass, then she must have been something of a miracle worker to the broken young men who had been brought to her ranch.

Mary had wanted to wrap her arms around Tony. She'd wanted to pull him into her and soothe the pain that had radiated out from his eyes, try to find and heal the little boy inside him who had been so badly damaged.

At the same time she'd realized the importance of maintaining some distance. She didn't in any way want to give him the impression that she might be open to another physical encounter. She could take care of his son and she could be his friend, but never anything more.

He'd taken two weeks of vacation time to be here as protection in the event that Ash Moreland made another attempt to take Joey. What if Ash made his next move in two weeks and two days? What if the evil man waited a month…or more?

As much as it would hurt Mary to say goodbye to the little boy who had captured her love, when Tony's vacation time was over, it was definitely time for him to make other arrangements.

She'd already allowed their agreement to go on far longer than she'd intended. It was time to put an end date to it. Hopefully, in the next two weeks Amy would be found, Ash Moreland would be in jail and then Tony and Amy could decide what was best for their child.

And what if Ash Moreland really was Joey's biological father? She shoved the familiar horrifying worry away. She only hoped the DNA test came soon and it showed that Tony was the father.

Tony might say he chose not to love, but there was no question he loved Joey, and Joey's best chance at a happy, loving future was with Tony.

Unable to stay in bed any longer, she decided to go ahead and get up and put on the morning coffee. It took her only minutes to brush her teeth and hair and then pull on a lightweight robe.

She opened her door, stepped out and immediately collided with Tony in the semi-darkened hallway. Her hand flew up to his broad, bare chest in an effort to steady herself and at the same time one of his hands grabbed hold of her shoulder.

"Whoa," he said softly and dropped his hand back to his side. In the faint illumination from the night-light plugged into a nearby wall socket, he looked hot as hell.

He was clad only in a pair of black boxers that hung low on his slim hips and he held his gun in one hand. His hair was loose and draped across his shoulders. He smelled of sleepy male and the lingering scent of his cologne.

"Sorry," she murmured. *Step back…drop your hand from his chest*, she told herself. But his skin was so wonderfully warm over his taut chest muscles.

"Good morning," he said.

His heartbeat resonated against her palm. Was her

heart beating as fast as his? Her cheeks burned with a blush and she yanked her hand away from him. "Good morning to you," she said briskly. "I was just on my way to make coffee."

"And I was just on my way to a shower," he replied.

"Then I'll see you in the kitchen in a few minutes." She sidestepped him and hurried up the hallway.

What was wrong with her? Why did he have the ability to evoke such longing in her? He made her feel like a giddy teenager eager for the high school quarterback to smile at her.

By the time the coffee was made, Tony walked into the kitchen only for Joey to give his familiar cry from the spare room.

"I'll go get him," Tony said.

It was hard to believe he was the same man who, two weeks ago, had stared at the baby with unabashed terror. He'd transformed. He was no longer afraid of taking care of Joey. He'd become confident in his role.

It was a good thing, she thought as she poured two cups of coffee and then pulled a bottle of formula out of the refrigerator. Fourteen more days and he was on his own. Fourteen more days and she had to tell him goodbye.

He came back into the kitchen and once again her breath caught in her throat. There was nothing sexier than a man wearing a gun to protect those he cared about and holding a smiling baby in his arms.

"He told me he's ready for his breakfast," Tony said.

"I'm ready for you both. I've got breakfast for a baby and a cup of coffee for Daddy."

"I think he looks like me," Tony said when they were seated at the table. He gazed down at the baby in his lap drinking his bottle and then looked at Mary. "Don't you think he looks like me?"

"He has dark hair like yours," she offered. But Ash Moreland also had black hair. It was obvious Tony wanted her to see a resemblance to him. "Maybe around the eyes," she finally said.

Tony smiled. "Yeah, that's kind of what I thought." Once again he gazed down at Joey. "I want to teach him to be strong and proud."

Halena swept into the kitchen clad in a flowing multicolored caftan and a little pink lace hat on her head. "How can you teach him to be proud when you know nothing about where you came from?" she asked with a stern look at Tony.

"Are you going somewhere?" he asked her. "You're wearing a hat."

"It's a hat kind of day," she replied and walked across the kitchen to get a cup of coffee. "Maybe you should wear your cowboy hat all day."

"It would just detract from my overall handsomeness," Tony replied with a twinkle in his eyes.

"You're all right, Tony Nakni," Halena replied with a grin.

Mary listened to the two of them with amusement. Tony had learned to give as well as he got when it came to Halena and there was no question her grandmother enjoyed their playful banter.

That banter continued through breakfast. Joey added his two cents with strings of baby gibberish that had them all laughing. "Since it's a hat day, I've decided not to start sewing today," Halena announced as they finished clearing the breakfast dishes.

"Then what are you going to do?" Mary asked.

"I have a new project to work on."

"Does that sound a bit scary or is it just me?" Tony asked, with that same twinkle of good humor in his eyes.

"You should be afraid, young warrior," Halena retorted.

"What kind of a project, Grandmother?" Mary asked.

"That's for me to know and you to find out. I'll be in my room if anyone needs me." She straightened her hat and then flounced out of the room.

"Has she always been this way?" Tony asked curiously.

"If you mean just a little bit crazy, then the answer is yes. She's always been eccentric, but she's getting more so with age."

"She must have been an interesting parental figure when you were growing up." He leaned down and placed the sleeping Joey in his bouncy chair.

"I'll admit there were times she mortified me, especially in my early teen years when almost everything mortified me. She'd show up to a school room party in a sparkly evening dress, or decide to do a traditional dance in the middle of the supermarket."

Tony smiled. "Somehow that sounds wonderful."

She nodded. "The really wonderful thing was that our home was the place where all my friends wanted to hang out. Grandmother would tell us scary stories about shadow beings who ate souls, or magical stories about the sun and the moon, Hashtahli and Hashi Ninak Anya, and their children, the stars. She always had snacks prepared for anyone who might show up and playing dress-up in her closet was the bomb. Even though I mourned the passing of my parents deeply, I was very blessed to have Grandmother in my life."

She eyed him with a new curiosity. "Whatever happened to Betty and Hank Ryan? Have you ever gone back to see them again?"

"Never. I have no idea if they're dead or alive. I have no intention of ever seeing them again. They are part of my past and have no place in my future."

"Do you know if they looked for you when you ran away?"

"I don't know for sure, but I doubt if they did." The darkness that had filled his eyes when he'd spoken about them the night before was absent, as if in telling his story to her some of that pain had vanished. "I'm sure they missed their whipping boy, but I doubt they wanted to get any law enforcement involved in my sudden absence."

"You should have gone to the police and told them about the abuse," Mary replied. It would have been nice to know that those vile people were at this very moment still spending time in jail.

"It never entered my mind to go to any authorities. Hank and Betty were white, the authorities were white and I had been told for years that I was nothing. I didn't think anyone would ever believe me about them."

"How do you feel about learning to make baskets?" she asked. A change in subject was definitely in order.

He gave her a warm smile. "I'm up for anything if you're a part of it."

"Then let's head out to the back porch. The sun is shining and it should be beautiful out there." She ignored the quick burst of heat that had suffused her at his words.

For the next two hours she taught Tony about the history and the making of the baskets that were a huge part of her business and an important part of Choctaw heritage.

When Joey awoke from his nap, they brought him out to the porch in his bouncy chair. As Mary dyed river cane, Tony kept Joey occupied by making funny faces and tickling him.

With the warm breeze caressing her face and baby giggles filling the air, Mary felt as complete as she'd ever been. If she was lucky, when Tony and Joey were gone, she'd occasionally dream-walk back to this place in time, where a profound happiness filled her heart.

It was almost dinnertime when Halena strode out onto the porch with a large handful of papers. She thrust the pile toward Tony, who took it in obvious confusion. "What's all this?" he asked.

"It's the education you missed out on when you were growing up," she replied.

Tony looked at Mary and she could tell he wondered if she'd told Halena about their conversation the night before. She shook her head and then shrugged.

"Every man with Choctaw blood should learn about

his roots and take pride in being a part of a people who have both dignity and courage. Now, you read all of that and I intend to quiz you about it later."

"And what if I get an answer wrong?" Tony asked.

"Then I'll make you wear this hat," Halena retorted and pointed up to the pink concoction perched atop her head. "Now, I'm feeling like tacos for dinner. I'm going to go get started on them."

"Is she serious about the hat?" Tony asked when she left the porch.

Mary grinned at him. "I wouldn't answer a question wrong if I was you. She'll sew it to your head while you're sleeping."

Tony laughed. "I'm shaking in my boots at the very thought."

"Why don't we head inside," Mary suggested a few minutes later. "It's starting to cool down and I should help with dinner."

"What can I do to help?" Tony asked as he picked up the bouncy chair where Joey was napping.

Mary gazed at him teasingly. "I think you should probably use all your spare time reading that material. You'd look terribly silly in that little pink hat." He laughed and together they went into the house.

Dinner was pleasant, and when it was finished, they all settled in to watch a movie. Halena got into the chair, leaving Mary to sit next to Tony on the sofa.

Anytime she was near him she felt as if all her senses were assaulted by him. His familiar scent evoked the memory of the hot, frantic lovemaking they'd shared. The languid slide of his gaze over her was pure temptation. It was as if unconsciously he was seducing her and she had to maintain her defenses against the desire he evoked inside her.

She put Joey down for the night and soon after that Halena waved a good-night as she headed to her bedroom. "I think I'm going to call it a night, too," Mary said.

Although it was fairly early, she felt uncharacteristically vulnerable. The day had been so good with Tony. He'd been so attentive as she'd worked and their conversations had been laced with laughter.

"I have to admit I'm a little tired myself," he replied. "Although I might do some reading before I go to sleep."

"Then I'll see you in the morning." A sense of relief accompanied her into her bedroom. As she dressed for bed, she chided herself for being so foolish.

She couldn't believe she was nervous about spending a couple hours alone in the living room with Tony. Where had her good sense gone?

She got into bed and squeezed her eyes closed, determined not to think about Tony Nakni, and hoping she didn't dream about him.

He was in the middle of a hot dream about Mary. They were both naked in her bed. Her full breasts filled his hands as they kissed with a passion so very hot he could smell the smoke, hear the snap and crackle of flames.

This time they moved slowly, exploring each other's bodies, indulging in a sensual foreplay that had been absent when they'd made love before. Bare skin sought bare skin and his mouth slid down her neck to capture one of her nipples. It leaped to attention in his mouth as she moaned.

She enflamed such a fire inside him the smoke from that fire choked in the back of his throat. He coughed... and tried to focus on their lovemaking. But he coughed again and suddenly awakened. Smoke filled the air.

Smoke... Fire!

The alarm finally registered in his brain, casting dreams away as fear sizzled through him. Something was burning. He jumped off the sofa. He pulled on his jeans, stepped into his boots, grabbed his gun from the coffee table and then went in search of the smoke source.

He didn't have to go far. The back porch was burning. Hungry flames ate the wood from the ground up and moved steadily toward the back door and the dining room area of the house.

They had to get out.

He had to get them all to safety.

He turned and rushed down the hallway and met Halena there. She held Joey in her arms and appeared like a ghostly wraith in the thin layer of smoke.

"Mary!" Tony turned into her bedroom, where she was apparently still asleep. "Mary, wake up!" He raced to the side of her bed, grabbed her by an arm and shook her.

Her eyes flew open and she shot up. "Tony, what's happening?"

"The house is on fire. Get some shoes on. We have

to get out." At that moment the smoke alarm in the kitchen began to shriek.

She flew out of bed, threw on her robe and stepped into a pair of sneakers at the foot of her bed. "Let's go."

They all headed to the living room, where Mary took Joey from Halena's arms and then gestured toward the front door.

"Wait," Tony said before she could reach the door. His brain whirled frantically. There was no way this was some sort of an accidental fire. There was nothing flammable on the back porch.

It had to be Ash.

Tony's blood ran cold despite the growing heat in the house. Ash had obviously set fire to the back porch, effectively leaving them no exit except for the front door.

He'd be waiting for them out there in the dark. Tony felt it in his gut. "Follow me," he said urgently. He led them back down the hallway and into Halena's bedroom at the back of the house.

He grabbed Mary by the shoulders. "I want you and Halena to get out the window and run for the woods in the backyard. Hide there until I come to get you, and if I don't come, then make your way to a neighbor's place and get help."

"Wait…what are you going to do?" she asked frantically. "Tony, aren't you coming with us?"

He opened the bedroom window and punched out the screen, a frantic fear torching through him. Was this the right decision? Was he sending them to safety or into a murderer's arms?

"Go," he said. He had nothing to trust but his instincts. He only prayed they were right.

"Come with us," Mary cried to him.

"Go," he repeated.

Halena ran over to the other side of the room and grabbed her naked-man wood carving off the wall and then stepped out of the window. She set the thick piece of wood onto the ground outside and then reached back in to take Joey from Mary. Mary gave Tony one more beseeching look and then she went outside.

The moment they were out of the house Tony raced back down the hallway and to the front door. His eyes burned from the thickening smoke in the living room and his heart pumped with adrenaline.

He held his gun tightly, unlocked the door and then opened it and somersaulted outside. Gunfire met him. He ran for the cover of the front of his truck in the driveway as bullets pinged all around him.

He reached the front fender and leaned against it, catching his breath as he tried to pinpoint Ash's location. He thought the man was hidden behind a bush across the street. Tony needed to keep him there until he was certain Mary and Halena had enough time to reach the woods and hide in the darkness.

He leaned out and fired off a few shots, shots that were met with return fire. Definitely behind the bush, he thought. The crackle of flames and the acrid scent of smoke in the air enraged him.

What the hell kind of man set fire to a house where there were two women and a baby inside? What kind of a monster went to such lengths?

Rage shortened his breaths as he once again leaned out and fired into the bush, hoping like hell that a bullet found the black heart of Ash.

There was no return fire.

The silence was more horrifying than the gunfire. Was he still behind the bush? If he wasn't, then where was he now? Had he realized that somehow the women had left the house by other means? Had he left his cover to run after them? Dear God, don't let him find the women!

Drawing a deep breath, Tony left the truck and ran toward the side of the house. He could only hope that Ash had realized his plan had failed and he had given up and left the area.

Still, Tony's heartbeat thundered in his ears as he ran toward the woods. Sirens filled the air, a welcome sign that somebody in the neighborhood had called for help.

The fire still burned, illuminating the area around the house in the back. He saw no sign of Ash. He'd just reached the dark woods when a fire engine and several police cars pulled up at the house.

He didn't care about the house. He didn't care about anything but getting to Mary and Halena and Joey and making sure they were okay. He still hadn't drawn any gunfire and his gut instinct told him Ash was gone, but he didn't want to take any chances.

If Ash hadn't left over his failed plan, then he surely would have fled at the first sign of the police. At least that was what Tony hoped.

Still, he wouldn't calm down until he found the women safe and sound. "Mary!" he cried. The woods were so dark and he had no idea what direction they might have run.

They had to be okay. If anything happened to any one of them, Tony would never be able to forgive himself, but he'd had no other option than to shove them out the window. Inside was the risk of fire and smoke inhalation and outside the front door had been a hail of bullets.

"Mary," he screamed.

And then she was there in front of him, Joey cradled in her arms and Halena by her side. He ran to Mary and threw his arms around her, unable to hide his relief.

"Thank God," he said and took a step back from them.

"And thank God you're okay," she replied with tears shining in her eyes. "We heard shots. We were so scared for you."

"I'm fine," he assured her. "The police have arrived, along with firefighters. We should be okay to head back to the house. Ash has to be gone now." He led them out of the trees.

"Tony? Mary?" Dillon stood in the backyard. Several firemen shot water from hoses on the last of the flames and the air felt heavy and oppressive with the lingering smoke.

"We're here," Tony shouted back.

Dillon met them in the middle of the yard. "I'm glad to see you're all okay. We got some calls about the fire and gunshots being heard. Several of my men have checked the area and as you can see the fire is almost out."

"It was Ash," Tony said grimly.

"The man is the worst kind of shadow being and he won't be satisfied until we're all dead and he has sucked out our souls," Halena said.

Tony didn't know anything about shadow beings, but a chill, a deep fear he'd never known before, raced up his spine at her words.

Chapter 10

As Tony continued to speak with Dillon about what had happened, Mary stared at her home. The porch was nothing more than a pile of blackened screen and smoldering wood. She couldn't even imagine what the inside of the house might look like.

At least it didn't look as if the fire had made its way inside, but there would be, at the very least, some smoke damage. She looked at Halena, who appeared older than she had hours before. Her gray hair was a tangled mess around her shoulders and the lines on her face seemed deeper. Still, she appeared stoic as she, too, stared at the damage.

Mary couldn't even begin to process the loss, or what measures would have to be taken to put things right again. She reminded herself that she held the most important thing in her arms.

The other things were just stuff, and stuff could be replaced. She was just grateful that they'd all gotten out of the house and were safe.

"We can't stay here," Halena finally said, stating the obvious. She held her wood carving as tightly to her chest as Mary held Joey. "We could go to Mabel's. She has plenty of room for us."

"No, I don't want to bring this danger to anyone else," Mary replied. "We'll go to the motel. Unless you want me to give Joey to Tony and tell him we're out of all this." She gazed at Halena. Joey fussed and Mary quickly rocked him in her arms to soothe him.

Halena drew herself up and lifted her chin. "We'll see this through together. Our little warrior needs all the help he can get."

Mary breathed a sigh of relief. Despite the danger, in spite of the carnage that the night had brought, she still wasn't ready to walk away. She was in this until the bitter end.

Tony left Dillon and walked back to where Mary and Halena stood. "We can't get back in the house tonight," he said. "Dillon is going to post a couple of men here so that there's no possibility of looting until we can get the back door replaced."

His features were shadowed, but his body radiated tension. "Mary, now is the time for you and Halena to walk away from all this. I never meant to involve you in something so dangerous. I had no idea what Amy was getting us into. We're lucky that the only casualty tonight was your porch and nothing worse."

"Listen…do you hear the leaves on the trees?" Halena held a hand to her ear. "They're telling me that it's not time to say goodbye to Tony Nakni and his son." She dropped her hand back to her side. "You aren't in this alone. We stand beside you."

Tony was silent for several long moments, as if their commitment to him and Joey left him speechless.

"We can go to the motel," Mary offered as a solution to where they'd stay.

"No, I'll take you to the ranch until we get this place cleaned up. You'll be safe there and we'll have all the cowboys there to make sure of it. I'll just make a quick call to Cassie."

He stepped aside as Jim Browbeck, the chief of the volunteer fire department, approached Mary and Halena. "As you can see, the fire is out. It was obviously arson and I believe the accelerant was nothing more complicated than gasoline poured on the porch and then lit."

"How bad is the damage?" Halena asked.

"It was mostly contained to the porch, but the kitchen and living room have some smoke damage."

"Is there any way to get into one of the bedrooms to grab some things for the baby?" Mary asked. There wouldn't be any stores open at this time of the night. Joey needed diapers and his formula.

"Tell me exactly what you need and where it is in the house and I'll send one of my men in," Jim replied. "It's still too hot for either one of you to enter."

She told him where the diaper bag was located and asked for whatever bottles were in the refrigerator. All they needed to do was make it through the rest of the night until the stores opened in the morning.

By the time Jim returned with the requested items, Tony had called Cassie and they were all set to head to the ranch. Dillon joined them at Tony's truck.

"I'll have Officer Goodall follow you out to Cassie's place," he said.

"Thanks, I appreciate it," Tony replied.

"Tony, this guy is obviously escalating," he said in a low voice. "I'll do everything on my end to catch this guy and I'll let the Oklahoma City authorities know what happened here tonight, but you need to continue to watch your back."

"We'll have lots of people watching our backs at the ranch," Tony replied.

"Can we get to this ranch now? This old woman has had enough excitement for one night and now just longs for a bed," Halena exclaimed impatiently.

Mary looked at her worriedly. Halena always appeared so strong and capable, but she wasn't a young woman anymore and now she'd been uprooted from her home under horrible circumstances.

"I'm fine," Halena said as if reading Mary's mind. "I'm just tired, as I'm sure we all are."

"Let's get moving," Tony replied.

Within five minutes they were all loaded into his truck and on their way to the Holiday ranch. Mary had no idea what to expect. She'd never officially met Cassie

Peterson, although she'd occasionally seen the pretty blonde in town.

How long could they stay at the ranch before Cassie got tired of them? What had to be done to get the house back in order so they could all return home?

And when would Ash Moreland strike again?

The ride was silent. Halena sat in the back with Joey, while Mary was in the passenger seat. Her gaze kept going to Tony. His mouth was a thin slash, a deep furrow rode his forehead and his broad shoulders were rigid.

She hadn't really processed until now that he was bare-chested. He hadn't taken the time to pull on a shirt. Thank God he'd awakened when he had, otherwise they might all have succumbed to smoke inhalation or Ash might have entered the house and killed them all and taken Joey.

As he drove, he kept his attention divided between the road before them and the rearview mirror, where the police car followed them.

She stared out the passenger window. At this point it didn't matter whether Joey was his biological son or not. Joey was an innocent baby who needed to be protected. So far, according to Dillon, Amy wasn't in any of the hospitals and she wasn't in the morgue. So, where was she?

Was Ash Moreland really Joey's biological father? Had Amy lied about Tony being the baby's daddy? Certainly if Amy loved Joey, she wouldn't have wanted a man like Ash to raise him.

A headache blossomed across her forehead with all

the gnawing questions pounding without answers. She sat up straighter in the seat as they drove through the entrance to the ranch.

A huge two-story house beamed light from all the windows despite the lateness of the night. Tony drove down the driveway around to the back of the house and parked.

Cassie Peterson stepped out on the back porch, her blond hair gleaming in the artificial porch light and a smile of welcome on her pretty face.

Despite the smile, nerves suddenly jangled inside Mary as they all got out of the car. They were definitely a motley crew. Halena wore a pair of neon-green sleep pants and a bright purple T-shirt advertising beer and clutched a piece of wood with a naked man on horseback. Mary was in her nightgown and robe and Tony wore only his jeans and his gun belt.

It was a wonder Cassie didn't run back into her house and lock the door. Instead she stepped off the porch to greet them.

"Come inside," she said, and to Mary's surprise she wrapped an arm around Mary's shoulders. "You'll be safe here."

Halena carried her carving and Tony grabbed the diaper bag and together they all entered the back door into a large kitchen. Official introductions were made as Cassie gestured them to sit at the round oak table.

"We can't thank you enough for allowing us to stay here," Mary said.

"I'd love to sit here and make nice conversation, but

I'd love it even more if you'd point me to the nearest bed," Halena said to Cassie.

"Of course." Cassie jumped up from the table and gestured for Halena to follow her. "I'll be right back," she said over her shoulder.

"I should have seen this coming," Tony said darkly when the two women had left the kitchen.

"How could you have known that he'd be crazy enough to set the house on fire?" Mary shook her head. "It was a dangerous move that might have killed the baby he seems to want so desperately. There was no way you could have seen this coming."

Tony looked down at Joey, who was peacefully sleeping in his car seat. When Tony gazed back at her, his eyes were narrowed and dark. "I don't care who his father is. Ash Moreland will never have him. I'll do whatever necessary legally or illegally to see that he doesn't spend a minute with Joey."

How far he'd come from the man who had professed that he never wanted children, she thought. He would go to the ends of the earth for the little boy who had been dropped at his doorstep. His commitment to Joey nearly stole her breath away with its intensity.

Cassie came back into the kitchen. "Your grandmother is in the first room on the right when you go up the stairs. The room across the hall has a queen-size bed and a crib is set up and ready for the little guy."

Tears suddenly blurred Mary's vision. The stress of the night slammed into her and raw emotions pressed against her chest and burned behind her eyes. Cassie's kindness and thoughtfulness only made her more emotional.

"I'm sorry," she said as she swiped the errant tears that trekked down her cheeks. "I guess I'm more tired than I realized."

"Why don't I go ahead and take you upstairs where you can get settled in. Tony can fill me in on anything I need to know and you and I can talk more in the morning."

Fifteen minutes later Mary was in the beautiful bedroom with Joey asleep in the crib and a fresh nightgown of Cassie's laid out at the foot of the bed for her use.

When she went into the bathroom to wash away the night's horror, she could hear Tony's and Cassie's soft murmurs drifting up the stairs.

Cassie was a petite little thing and the nightgown barely covered Mary's behind. However, it smelled of fresh-scented fabric softener and Mary was grateful to get out of her own clothes. She didn't know if her clothing really smelled of smoke or if she just imagined it.

Ready for bed, she walked over to the bedroom window and peered outside. The darkness of night cloaked everything. Were they really safe here?

The question thundered in her heart. Was this the safe haven they needed? How long would Cassie allow them to stay here? Hopefully, with this newest threat, the officials in Oklahoma City would step up their game in an effort to find Ash and get him in jail.

She couldn't see an ending to this no matter how hard she tried. She didn't even know what a happy ending would look like in this situation. She walked over to the crib and gazed down at the little boy at the heart of everything.

Tears once again burned at her eyes. *Go to bed*, she commanded herself. *At least for the rest of the night you're all safe here.*

She just feared what tomorrow might bring.

Tony jerked awake with fight-or-flight adrenaline surging through his body. His heart pumped rapidly as he shot up and reached blindly for his gun. It took him several seconds to register that he was on Cassie's sofa in her great room.

He'd crashed here because he hadn't wanted to go to his bunk room and leave the house unguarded for the night with just the women inside.

Dawn light seeped into the windows and he drew several deep breaths to get his heartbeat back to a more normal rhythm. He'd gotten only a couple of hours of sleep, but there was no way he was going back to sleep now that he was awake.

A lot of things had to happen today. Halena and Mary needed clothes, Joey would need more diapers and formula and something had to be done about Mary's house.

He intended to take care of the house. He was the reason it had been set on fire. Hopefully, he could either hire someone to do the work, or get some of his fellow cowboys to tear down what was unsalvageable and rebuild things the way they had been. He'd hire a company to clean up any smoke and water damage and he'd pay for any of the basket supplies and other items Mary had lost on the porch.

Damn Ash Moreland. He was like an evil shadow in the night, a phantom who moved through the world without leaving any footprints behind.

Where was he staying? Why couldn't the police locate him? If he'd been on their radar as a suspected murderer, surely they knew some of the places he might go to hide out.

He got up from the sofa and rubbed a hand down his face. He needed to get to his bunk room and get some clean clothes, but in the meantime he wanted coffee.

The house was quiet and he was surprised when he padded into the kitchen and found Halena seated at the table. "Halena, I didn't know you were awake," he said in surprise.

"I can move very quietly when I want to," she replied. "Besides, you were busy sleeping with your mouth open and catching flies when I walked by you."

"Was I snoring?" he asked.

"Not when I passed you."

"Good, now I'm going to see if I can find the coffee and get a pot going." He moved to the cabinet above the coffeemaker. "Bingo." He took out a can of coffee and a filter.

It took him only minutes to get the coffee brewing and then find two cups for them to use. "Did you sleep at all?" he asked.

"A bit," she replied. "Enough that I dream-walked for a little while."

"Where did you go?" Tony leaned with his backside against the counter as he waited for the coffee to finish brewing.

She frowned. "I don't know. It was a strange place where the moon wept and the stars spun crazily in the sky. I think it was telling me the turmoil isn't over yet, that there are more bad times to come."

"Hopefully not," Tony replied, although he knew in his gut that Ash wasn't finished with them yet. He turned to pour the coffee and then joined her at the table. "I'm hoping that we'll be safe here and sooner rather than later Ash Moreland will be behind bars."

Halena took a sip of her coffee and her eyes twinkled over the top of the cup. "Are all the cowboys here as handsome as Clay and Sawyer?" she asked when she lowered her cup.

"Halena, I believe you have more than a little bit of cougar in you," he replied.

"I just like to look…and occasionally pinch."

Tony couldn't help but laugh.

"And what's so funny in here?" Cassie came into the kitchen clad in a blue robe that was the exact color of her eyes.

"Nothing that should be repeated," Halena replied with a pointed look at Tony.

"Ah, I'm so glad you made coffee," Cassie said as she beelined to the counter. "Occasionally Adam comes in early and has the coffee ready when I get up."

"Adam is the ranch foreman," Tony explained to Halena.

"He's been a godsend since I inherited this place. I didn't know anything about ranching when I first arrived." Cassie poured herself a cup of coffee and then joined them at the table. "Now, what do we have on the agenda today and what can I do to help?"

"You've helped enough just by allowing us to stay here," Halena replied.

"This house has been a safe haven for several women since I've been here," Cassie replied.

"Everything happened so fast last night we escaped with just the clothes on our backs. The first order of business is to get some clothes for Halena and Mary and also get some supplies for Joey." Tony frowned.

It was possible that the clothes in the bedrooms could be washed and be okay, but he hated the idea of taking the two women and Joey back there without some backup. He gazed at Cassie. "I'd appreciate it if a couple of the men could go to Mary's house with us to get some things."

"No problem," Cassie replied. "Take Sawyer and Flint with you. You can leave Joey here with me if you're comfortable with that."

Halena stared at her for a long moment and then nodded. "We would be comfortable with that. I know you'll take good care of the baby."

"Absolutely," Cassie agreed.

"It shouldn't take us long," he said.

"What shouldn't take us long?" Mary came into the kitchen wearing the robe she'd had on the night before. Joey was bright-eyed in her arms. Tony immediately jumped up to take the baby from her.

Joey fussed, indicating he was ready for his morning meal. Mary poured herself a cup of coffee and Tony got a bottle from the refrigerator.

"We were talking about going back to the house to get some clothes and whatever else you two might need for your stay here," Tony said. Joey curled up in his arms and gazed at him with happy eyes as he chugged on his bottle.

"We definitely need some things," Mary said. Her eyes were dark and troubled. "Do you think it's safe to go back there?"

"We'll leave Joey here with Cassie and we'll take a couple of men with us. It should be fine," Tony assured her. With a couple of cowboys watching their backs, Tony felt more comfortable.

"I might be able to find something for you both to wear today," Cassie said. "I'm sure you don't want to run around wearing a robe and…and…" Her gaze shot to Halena. "And whatever," she finally said.

For the next fifteen minutes they talked about the logistics of the trip back to Mary's house and then Cassie got up to make pancakes.

Halena insisted she help and as the two worked together to prepare breakfast Tony and Mary remained seated at the table. The conversation continued as to the day's plans.

As they ate, the women visited and got to know each other better. Tony remained silent and listened to the female chatter. Thank God Cassie was like the aunt she'd been named after, he thought. She had a warm and giving heart and never turned away anyone who was in trouble.

Surely, Ash wouldn't make a move on them here, where they were surrounded by armed men who would protect what was theirs with their lives. And Joey and Mary and Halena would be claimed by all of them because they meant something to Tony.

How could Dillon even think that one of the cowboys here was a murderer? They were Tony's brothers, the men he knew he could depend on whenever things got bad.

He shoved this thought away as Adam Benson came in the back door. "Good morning," he said in obvious surprise at the sight of all of them. "Looks like things have changed a lot since the time I told you good-night last night," he said to Cassie.

"Ash set Mary's house on fire," Tony said.

As the three women cleared off the breakfast dishes, Tony filled Adam in on what had happened the night before. "So, what do you need from all of us?" Adam asked when Tony had finished.

"In the short term Cassie said Sawyer and Flint could go with us to Mary's home so we can pick up a few things. In the longer term I'd like everyone to look out for anyone who doesn't belong on the property, especially around the house," Tony replied. "This man is dangerous, Adam."

"He's a shadow being from hell," Halena insisted.

"Then we'll make sure he doesn't get anywhere near here," Adam replied firmly. "We'll set up a couple of guards to work the nights here at the house. I'll coordinate with the men to take care of it."

"Won't the men mind having extra work?" Mary asked worriedly.

"Not these men," Adam assured her. "We take care of each other."

Arrangements were made for them to leave the house at nine. Tony walked out the back door with Adam and headed toward the cowboy motel, where he could take a quick shower and get into clean clothes.

"I'll just hang around here until you come back," Adam said and sat on one of the lawn chairs near the side of the porch.

Tony flashed him a grateful smile. Although it was hard to believe Ash might make a move so early this morning after last night's activities, he'd rather be safe than sorry. "I won't be long."

He hurried toward his bunk room. The other men would already be up and out in the pastures, or in the barn or stable taking care of the daily chores.

He wouldn't be completely at ease until they were all back here and really settled in. There was no way Ash would get past the men who would now be looking for any sign of him here. There was no way he'd get close enough to grab Joey or do harm with all the cowboys on guard.

It took him only twenty minutes to shower and change clothes. He placed a call to Jim Browbeck, who agreed to meet them at Mary's place, and then Tony headed back to the big house.

At nine o'clock they headed toward town and the scene of the unexpected fire the night before. Mary wore a pink T-shirt and a pair of gray jogging pants that hit her midcalf. Halena was clad in a long summery dress in muted colors. It was the most normal thing Tony had ever seen the old woman wear and she expressed several times about how much she hated it.

"Jim is meeting us at your house," he told them. "I thought it would be a good idea to have him around in case there were still hot embers or places of potential structural danger."

"That's probably a good idea. We really just need to grab a few articles of clothing. Hopefully, I can make arrangements to get the house fixed as soon as possible," Mary replied.

"I'll take care of the house repairs. I don't want you to worry about it," Tony said firmly. "All you have to worry about for the next couple of days is taking care of each other."

"And keeping Grandmother away from the cowboys," Mary said under her breath with a touch of humor.

Tony flashed her a smile, grateful for the ease of the tension that had been an undercurrent throughout the morning.

Jim Browbeck was already there when they got to Mary's house, as was Officer Juan Ramiriz, who was chatting with the fire chief on the front porch.

"Good morning," Tony said to them both.

"Good morning to you. I've already been inside and got a good look around," Jim said after they had all greeted each other. "The fact that the fire was set on the exterior wall of the back porch was actually a good thing. The porch is destroyed, along with the back door leading into the house, but the structure is sound and things don't look nearly as grim this morning in the light of day."

Mary released an audible sigh. "So, we can get some items from inside?"

"That won't be a problem. The main thing the house needs is a new back door and some painting and cleanup in the kitchen, dining room and living room. The bedrooms are virtually untouched. I don't even think much smoke got to those rooms," he replied.

"Dillon said he'd keep a man on the house until you can get a new back door so the place can be properly locked up," Juan said.

"I'll see to the door later this afternoon," Tony replied. "You can tell Dillon it will be fixed by nightfall. Now, let's get this done."

Sawyer and Flint stood near the street in front of the house, on guard for anything that might come their way. Although Tony didn't expect trouble, he was grateful for their presence.

Since Mary hadn't had a chance to grab her purse the night before and didn't have her house key, they all went around back to enter.

"I made a little path through the rubble for you to get inside," Jim said.

"Thank you," Mary replied, her voice soft and sober.

They entered into the kitchen and then walked into the living/dining room area. There was a faint scent of smoke and the walls were going to need repainting, but thankfully it was all just cosmetic issues.

Halena disappeared down the hallway into her bedroom. Tony turned to Mary. "Why don't you pack up your things and I'll load a suitcase full of Joey's items."

Her face was pale and her eyes were slightly glassy,

as if memories of the night before took hold of her. "Mary?" he said softly.

Her shoulders snapped straight and her eyes focused in on him. She lifted her chin and gave him a curt nod. "Let's get to it."

It took Tony only a few minutes to fill the suitcase Amy had left with Joey. He not only included clothes, but also any cans of formula and extra diapers that were in the room.

"I'm going to carry this out to the car and then come back in for the bouncy chair and the playpen," he said to Mary.

She looked up from the suitcase she had opened on her bed. "Since Cassie has a crib, don't worry about getting the playpen."

Halena came down the hallway with a huge suitcase and sporting a large hat with a purple feather in it. "You never know when you'll need a purple hat," she said to Tony.

Tony fought desperately against an unexpected burst of laughter that threatened to bubble out of him. He had a feeling that no matter what dire things might happen, Halena would meet them with her own brand of aplomb and a fancy hat on her head.

"I'll take your suitcase," he said. Halena handed it to him and then she went into Mary's bedroom while he went out to his truck.

As he waited for Mary to finish up, he sat on the sofa in the living room. Even though he believed they'd be safe at the ranch, he couldn't help the worries that flittered through his brain.

Things couldn't get back to normal until Ash was arrested and would face charges of attempted kidnapping and perhaps arson if Dillon found any evidence that could be used against him in tying him to the fire.

There was no way Tony believed the man was finished with them. He was obviously obsessed with getting Joey into his possession. Tony just wished he knew what Ash's next move would be.

Twenty minutes later they were loaded up and were saying goodbye to Juan and Jim when Dillon pulled up. Tony's stomach muscles bunched with tension as he watched the lawman get out of his car and approach them.

Dillon's eyes were dark, and he offered them no smile. Mary stepped closer to Tony, as if she, too, had a sense of deep foreboding.

"I stopped by the ranch and Cassie told me you were here getting some things," he said.

"Do you have news about Ash?" Tony asked.

Dillon shook his head. "Not Ash… Amy."

"What about her?" Dread pooled in the pit of Tony's stomach.

Dillon drew in a deep breath. "She was found in a motel room just outside of Oklahoma City late last night. She's dead—she was stabbed to death."

Mary gasped and a sharp feeling of grief swept through Tony, along with a deep arctic chill. Knowing somebody was a suspected murderer was one thing, but believing that person had stabbed to death somebody you knew was absolutely horrifying.

"Ash," Tony said flatly.

"The investigation is only in the early stages," Dillon replied.

"Ash believes Joey is his, so if he killed Amy, then he killed the mother of his three-month-old son." Mary stared at Tony, her eyes filled with the darkness that seeped into Tony's soul. "He's the worst kind of monster," she said softly. "And he's coming after us."

Chapter 11

The news of Amy's murder ached inside Mary's heart. The blond-haired sprite who had been such a part of Mary's childhood was now gone forever. Amy wouldn't appear one day on her doorstep, full of regrets about using again, swearing that she was going to do better and begging for Mary to not be mad at her.

Memories rushed through her head. The laughter of the slumber parties they'd had rang inside her head. They'd painted each other's fingernails and experimented with makeup. They'd talked about boys and how gross they thought it would be if a man put his tongue in their mouths while kissing.

They had been young and so innocent, but Amy's innocence had fled far too quickly. By the time she was sixteen she was already dabbling with drugs and sleeping with different guys.

Mary had always feared for Amy's life, but she'd assumed she would self-destruct. She'd never dreamed she'd be murdered, bringing forth Mary's worst fears.

Joey no longer had a mother, and if Tony really was the father, then he would not have a partner to help in raising the little boy.

They drove back to the ranch in silence, but in Mary's head she heard the sounds of Joey's cooing and gurgling. The sound of his happiness ringing in her brain only made everything more tragic.

Protect him from evil. Those had been Amy's last words to Tony, and Mary knew without a doubt that Tony would do everything in his power to honor them. Tony would take care of Joey, but who would take care of Tony?

When they reached the ranch house, Cassie was on the back porch, her face somber. "Dillon told me about Amy," she said to Tony. "I'm so sorry for your loss."

"Thanks, Cassie," he replied, equally as somber. "Why don't you women head on inside and I'll unload everything."

Mary and Halena followed Cassie back into the house and into the great room, where Joey was asleep on a blanket on the floor. "Sit and relax for a few minutes," Cassie said. She sat in one of the chairs.

Mary eased down next to Halena on the sofa. "I like your hat," Cassie said to Halena.

The old woman reached up and straightened it on her head. "I like hats, especially on bad days. A good hat can make you feel better. But I also like hats on good days, too."

Tony came in carrying two suitcases. "I'll just take these upstairs to the bedrooms and go back out to get the rest of the things."

"I'm sad for Amy, but I'm not surprised that she had a bad end," Halena said softly as she gazed at Joey. "May she rest in peace. At least she won't be tormented any longer."

She stood. "And now I'm going to go ahead and unpack." She headed for the stairs.

"I'm so sorry about Amy," Cassie said once Halena had disappeared from sight. "What a horrible thing."

Mary nodded. "She had a good heart, but she was a troubled woman who made bad choices. Still, she didn't deserve what happened to her."

"Nobody deserves that," Cassie replied. "I'll bet your grandmother is a fascinating person."

Mary smiled and realized Cassie had changed the subject on purpose. "She's definitely unique."

"She has a beautiful face. I'd love to paint her sometime."

"You paint?"

It was Cassie's turn to smile. "Yes, I paint when I have spare time. I dreamed of being an artist on the streets of New York City, selling my paintings out of the most prestigious art galleries." She released a deep sigh. "It's strange where fate takes you."

Mary gazed down at the sleeping baby. "Yes, it's definitely strange." She looked back at Cassie. "But it wasn't fate that brought us here. It was the evil doings of a tin man."

"A tin man?"

Mary nodded. "A man without a heart…a man without a soul." She wrapped her arms around her shoulders in an effort to warm the chill that filled her as she thought of Ash Moreland…the man she was certain had murdered Amy.

Cassie leaned forward and her blue eyes shone with conviction. "Mary, that tin man can't hurt you here. We're all going to make sure of that."

Gazing into Cassie's earnest eyes, Mary almost believed it, but not quite. She couldn't shake the notion that they weren't out of the woods yet. Until Ash was in jail the danger was still very real.

A half an hour later Mary was in the bedroom unpacking her clothes. Her grandmother had been right the morning she'd told Mary about her dream walk to Kansas with a tornado and a tin man.

She'd seen great change and danger from a man—too bad she hadn't seen a fire, a murder and complete upheaval in their world. Too bad she hadn't seen how this would all end.

Tony had left with a couple of men to return to the house and see about installing a new back door. He'd also told her before he left that he'd have the porch rebuilt and the interior walls painted.

At the moment she didn't care about the house. All she cared about was the little boy who was reaching up to bat at the old, slightly faded mobile Cassie had hung over his crib.

She hung her T-shirts and the other blouses she'd packed in the closet and then placed her jeans and underpants in the dresser drawers, then sat on the edge of the bed and stared unseeingly toward the window.

Amy was gone forever and Tony wasn't the marrying type. Would he change his tune so that Joey would have a mother figure in his life? Every child needed a soft place to fall.

She hoped and prayed that before Joey got too old Tony would find a good woman and fall in love. She wanted Joey to have a mother who would kiss his booboos and tears away, a mom who would bake cookies and throw birthday parties and tuck him into bed each night with a story and a lullaby. She wished that woman could be her, but she knew it wasn't.

Damn cancer.

Damn it to hell and back.

Hot tears burned at her eyes, tears she swallowed hard against. It had robbed her of everything meaningful in her life. It had taken her mother. It had taken her only aunt.

It had stolen Mary's dreams of a family of her own. It had forced her to make a decision that would assure she would never know a man's love.

Damn cancer.

She jumped up from the bed. It was ridiculous for her to sit here and feel sorry for herself. She was finished with pity parties.

She walked over to the crib. Joey had fallen asleep. Motherless child, now that was a real tragedy, she thought.

She left the room and headed downstairs, needing something or somebody to pull her out of her own head. Tony would see to it that Joey thrived and she reminded herself that she was so much more than what cancer had done to her.

Cassie was in the kitchen and greeted her with a pleasant smile. "Sit and talk to me while I wrestle with this chicken for dinner," she said.

"Need some help?" Mary asked. "The last thing we want is to make more work for you, Cassie."

"Please, just relax. I've got this," Cassie assured her. "Do you want something to drink?"

"No, I'm good." Mary sat at the table and watched as Cassie washed the whole chicken in the sink and then shoved it into a bag.

"I love bag cooking," she said. "You throw in a hunk of protein and some vegetables and then put it in the oven and that's it."

"Do you like to cook?" Mary asked.

Cassie turned up her pert nose. "Not really. I might like it if I knew more about it. When I was living in New York, I almost never turned on my oven or stove. There was a deli right down the street where I bought all my meals. It wasn't until I moved here that I realized if I didn't cook, then I didn't eat…and I do love to eat."

"While we're here, if you just give the word, I'm sure Grandmother would be pleased to teach you some things about cooking. She loves to cook."

"Really? I'll bet she's an awesome cook." Cassie began to shove peeled potatoes and carrots into the bag with the chicken. She tied the bag, then opened the oven and put the baking pan inside.

"Now, how about a cup of hot tea?" she said. "I always enjoy a nice cup of tea around this time of the day."

"That sounds good," Mary agreed.

Maybe a cup of tea would erase all the concerns that floated around in her head. She wondered what Tony was doing at the house, she worried about what Ash would do next and she was aware of the ticking clock that would end her involvement with both Tony and Joey when Tony's vacation time was over.

Cassie set a cup of tea in front of her and then got the sugar bowl, some slices of lemon and a small pitcher of milk. She then poured a cup for herself and joined Mary at the table.

"Tell me about your business. Tony told me you make all kinds of beautiful things."

Mary looked at the attractive blonde with gratitude. She knew what she was doing—she was trying to get Mary's mind off the issues that faced them all. It worked. Cassie was not only a good listener, but also asked all kinds of questions and appeared genuinely interested in how Mary made a living.

"I can't wait to get on my laptop and check out your site," she said. "You're obviously quite an artist yourself."

"Speaking of being an artist, tell me more about your paintings," Mary said.

"I mostly like working with oils, although occasionally I'll dabble a bit with watercolors. I always painted cityscapes until I moved here. Now I'm starting to dabble in country paintings." Cassie stopped talking as Halena came into the kitchen.

Her purple hat was gone, as was the dress that Cassie had found for her to wear. Instead Halena wore leopard-print baggy trousers with a pink camo T-shirt.

"Grandmother, Cassie doesn't know much about cooking. Maybe while we're here you could share some of your special recipes with her and show her how to do them," Mary said.

Halena eyed Cassie as if she was a peculiar bug she'd never seen before. "How did you get to be your age and not know much about cooking?"

"Before I came to Bitterroot I ate out a lot," Cassie replied. She leaned back in her chair and smiled at Halena. "You know, I think I have a few hats upstairs from New York City that I could give you in exchange for some cooking lessons."

Halena narrowed her gaze and then nodded. "Bribery... I like it. You've got a deal."

"We can start tomorrow night, since dinner for this evening is already in the oven," Cassie said.

For the next hour the women chatted about everything from the working of the ranch to people in town they all knew. The conversation halted long enough for Mary to race up the stairs to check on Joey, who was awake and hollering for attention. She changed his diaper and then carried him down the stairs and returned to the kitchen, where she deposited him at her feet in his bouncy chair.

"You are such a sweetheart," Cassie said to Joey, who

babbled and grinned at her in return. "I think you're the cutest baby I've ever seen."

"Why don't you have a man and a baby of your own?" Halena asked.

"Grandmother…" Mary shot her a warning look.

"What?" Halena looked at her innocently. "I can't help my curiosity. It's pretty much all you have left when you get to be my age."

"It's okay," Cassie replied with a glint of good humor in her eyes. "I don't have a man or a baby because I'm still trying to find myself."

Halena raised an eyebrow. "That sounds like some New Age crap to me. You're a pretty woman and I'd think all the cowboys in the area would be after you. Are you a lesbian?"

"Grandmother!" Mary was outraged and worried. Dear God, all they needed was for her outspoken grandmother to get them kicked off the ranch.

Cassie laughed uproariously. "Oh, I'm going to enjoy having the two of you here. And no, I'm not a lesbian." She grabbed a napkin from the table and wiped her eyes as Mary breathed a sigh of relief.

"I'm not even dating at the moment," Cassie continued. "Right now I don't know if my forever home is going to be this place or back in New York City, so I've put my love life on hold for now."

"Why would you want to go back to New York City?" Halena asked.

Cassie shrugged her shoulders. "To fulfill the dreams I have for myself."

"You have a beautiful home and a successful ranch

that probably makes you more money than you know what to do with. You have all those cowboys with their broad shoulders and sexy butts working for you. I'd say you should just change your dreams," Halena said.

Cassie smiled and before she could reply Joey began to fuss. Mary got up to fix him a bottle. While she fed him, the conversation changed to what kinds of meals Halena intended to teach Cassie how to cook.

"You definitely need to know how to make an enchilada pie and chili. Those are real man-pleasers and they'll come in handy when you find yourself and get a man in your life," Halena said.

"That sounds good," Cassie replied. "And maybe you can teach me how to cook a good roast. It seems like mine is always tough."

The food chatter continued until around four o'clock, when Tony came in the back door and greeted them all with a tired smile. He sat at the table in the chair across from Mary.

"We managed to load up and take away what was left of your porch and we got a new back door installed," he said. "I left a message for Frankie Brale to see if he can take care of the painting on the inside and the rebuilding of the porch."

Frankie Brale was a handsome bald man who ran a successful home repair and renovation business. He had a reputation for being a hard worker and fair in pricing.

"Tony, I really don't expect for you to take care of all this. You let me know what it's going to cost and I'll write a check," Mary replied.

Tony looked down at Joey, who was napping in the

bouncy chair on the floor, and then he gazed back at Mary. "My son…and my problems, and the last thing I want is for you to come to any harm, financially or any other way. I've got this, Mary, and I've got it with pleasure."

His gaze was soft and held a touch of yearning. Oh, those beautiful eyes could get her in a whole lot of trouble if she didn't stay strong.

He got up from the table. "And now I'm going to head back to my bunk for a nice hot shower." He looked at Cassie. "Is it okay if I come back after dinner?"

"The more the merrier," Cassie replied.

With a nod of goodbye, Tony went back out the door. Cassie smiled at Mary. "Do you realize that man is head over heels in love with you?"

Mary's heart stuttered in her chest. "No, that's crazy. Tony doesn't love me and he's not in love with me. He just believes he needs me right now…because of Joey. He appreciates how I've helped him out, that's all."

Tony wanted her. There was no question that he'd like to have her in bed again, but love had nothing to do with it. He couldn't love her. She just wouldn't allow it.

Halena smiled at Cassie. "My granddaughter is a very foolish woman. Now, about those hats you mentioned earlier…"

Tony watched as several of Frankie's men unloaded lumber from the back of a truck. In the past three days the interior of the house had been repainted and now it was time for Frankie and his men to put back the porch where Mary had spent an afternoon teaching him about her basket weaving.

Tony was making the porch bigger and better than it had been. He hadn't told Mary yet, he wanted it to be a surprise. But besides increasing the size of the porch he was putting in glass and screens so that if she wanted she could work in the space throughout the whole year.

It was the very least he could do for the woman who had put her own life on hold to help him. It was the very least he could do for the woman who had captured his reluctant heart.

He leaned with his back against his truck's driver door, raised his face to the warm afternoon sun and then frowned as he thought about the past three days.

Mary and Halena seemed to have settled in nicely with Cassie. The three of them got along well and Cassie appeared to be enjoying the company of the two females and Joey.

Each evening one of the men went on guard duty, patrolling around the house and looking for trouble through the night. During the days Tony was inside the house playing with Joey or feeding him or putting him down for sleep in the crib.

What he hadn't been doing was spending any quality time alone with Mary. He missed the hours when Halena would retire for the night and he and Mary sat on her sofa and just talked.

Hell, who was he kidding? He not only missed those conversations, but he also missed tasting her lips and feeling her body warm against his own.

A fire in the dark and a tragic murder in a motel

room—nothing that had occurred had lessened his desire for Mary. And nothing that had happened over the last couple of days had cleared his confusion about what exactly she wanted from him.

She'd told him she didn't want a relationship with him and yet far too often he felt her gaze lingering on him. There was a heat in her eyes when she looked at him, an occasional wistful yearning there that made him believe she wanted him as badly as he wanted her.

He'd given her the opportunity to walk away from this whole mess more than once, but she hadn't walked. What had kept her with him? He didn't believe it was just her love and concern for Joey.

He mentally cursed himself for his own desires. With the potential danger that was a constant undercurrent in the air, was it any wonder she wasn't in the mood for romance?

Once again old feelings of inadequacy filled him. Was he just not good enough for her? Was he mistaken in thinking that she wasn't just staying for Joey, but for him as well? He just didn't know what to believe. All he knew was that he was grateful she was still in his life.

He'd called Dillon earlier that morning to get updates on Ash and on Amy's murder investigation. It was an understatement to say that he was disappointed with Dillon's report.

Ash was still on the loose, apparently hiding out someplace where the authorities hadn't been able to find him. The knife used to kill Amy had been found in the motel room but had yielded no fingerprints.

In fact, the entire room had been wiped down and

interviews with other guests and motel staff had also come up empty. The bottom line was that so far they had found no evidence to help them name a specific suspect in her murder. Tony didn't need evidence to know who was guilty.

He straightened up as Frankie approached him. "We should be able to get a frame up before nightfall," he said. "And then hopefully within a couple of days it should be done."

"Sounds good," Tony replied. "I'm going to head out. I'll check back in here tomorrow."

Minutes later he was in his truck and headed back to the ranch, his thoughts still filled with Mary. With a guard at the house, he was back sleeping in his bunk each night and having meals in the cowboy dining room.

Still, he spent every minute of the day that he could inside with the women and his boy. His boy…he prayed it would be so. The paternity test should come in the next couple of weeks and he was surprised by how badly he wanted Joey to be his biological child. And how badly he wanted Mary to be his woman.

He scarcely recognized himself anymore. Three weeks ago he was a confirmed bachelor who had no desire to share his life with anyone. It had taken a happy little boy, the telling of his childhood misery and the nearness of a strong, beautiful woman to shift his priorities and turn his life upside down in a positive way.

When he reached the ranch, he parked his truck in the shed and then walked up to the big house. Halena sat in a chair on the back porch talking with Sawyer.

The woman wore a silver sequined beret set at a cocky angle and Sawyer wore an expression of quiet, horrified fascination. Sawyer grinned in obvious relief as Tony approached them.

"Like the hat," Tony said.

Halena reached up and touched it with a satisfied smile. "It's from New York City. I showed Cassie how to make my enchiladas this afternoon and this handsome cowboy and I were just talking about sex."

"Uh...she was talking and I was mostly listening," Sawyer said hurriedly.

Tony decided to take pity on his friend. "I saw Adam down by the shed and he needs you to help him with something."

Sawyer gave him a grateful smile and then turned to Halena. "Guess I'd better go. It was nice talking to you."

Tony had never seen the man move so fast as he took off across the lawn. "Were you being a bit naughty?" Tony asked the old woman.

Halena smiled like a small girl caught with her hand in the cookie jar. "Perhaps a little. He has the most beautiful blushes. By the way, Cassie was kind enough to allow me to use her printer this afternoon. I left your homework on the coffee table inside. I have not forgotten your lack of education, Tony Nakni."

"I'll be sure and take it with me to my bunk room when I go in a few minutes, but in the meantime I need to go inside and check on your granddaughter and Joey."

"I'll just sit here a bit longer and see if I can entertain myself with another one of the cowboys here."

"Behave yourself," Tony said with a laugh, knowing she would do no such thing.

He entered the back door and immediately smelled the scent of the cooking enchiladas and heard the sound of female voices coming from the great room.

"Hello," he yelled, wanting them to know of his presence before he just appeared.

"In here, Tony," Cassie called from the great room.

He entered to see Cassie and Mary seated on the sofa and several paintings leaning against the wall. Joey was on his back on a blanket on the floor with his feet in his hands. When he saw Tony, he released his feet and waved his hands wildly with excitement.

Tony leaned down and picked him up. "Hey, little man, what's going on in here?" Joey wiggled in his arms.

"Cassie has been showing me some of her paintings," Mary said. "She's incredibly talented."

Cassie's face glowed with happiness. "We've come to an agreement and Mary is going to offer some of my Western-themed paintings for sale on her website."

"That's great," Tony replied and sat in a nearby chair with Joey on his lap.

"It definitely gives me the incentive to pick up the paintbrushes again," Cassie replied. "I haven't done much painting since Nicolette and Sammy were staying here with me."

"That's right, Nicolette married one of your ranch hands," Mary replied.

Cassie nodded. "Lucas Taylor. He was the first of the men to leave this ranch behind. Since then we've had another one leave. Forest Stevens ran off to Oklahoma City to be with his lady love. At least when Dusty and Nick found true love they didn't stop working here."

"Adam told us that you intend to hire on a couple of new men," Tony said.

"We've got four empty rooms in the cowboy motel and plenty of work for additional hands," Cassie replied. "I've got an ad for help wanted running in the paper starting next week."

"It will be kind of strange to have new men here." Tony shifted Joey from one thigh to the other. "It's always just been the twelve of us. But it's been strange since Lucas and Forest stopped working here."

"Life brings changes," Halena said from the doorway. "The real mark of strength comes in how you adapt to the changes."

"And with that piece of wisdom, I'd better get to the dining room. Cookie hates it when we show up late to eat." Tony gave Joey a kiss on the cheek and then placed him back on the blanket.

"Mary, want to walk out with me?" he asked as he picked up the pile of papers Halena had printed for him. He found himself holding his breath, just hoping for a couple of minutes of private time with her.

"Okay," she agreed. She got up and together they walked through the kitchen and out the back door.

"Frankie thinks he'll have things finished at the house in the next couple of days," he said once they were outside.

She sank down on the chair where Halena had been sitting earlier. "I guess that's good news, right?"

"Your house will be repaired, but that doesn't mean I want us moving back in there right now. We're far safer here and I'd like us all to remain here until Ash is finally arrested."

"And what if weeks go by…months pass and he still isn't in jail?" Her beautiful brown eyes stared at him intently. "Tony, we can't stay here forever and once your vacation time is finished I think you need to find other arrangements for Joey."

He'd known this was coming. He'd feared that eventually she'd want out. This had never been her problem. In doing him a favor she'd become embroiled in a dangerous drama she'd never asked for. What he hadn't expected was the sharp stab of pain in his heart, the almost breathless feeling her words caused him.

He wanted to tell her how he felt about her. He wanted her to know that he loved her, but there was a distance in her eyes that kept the words trapped deep inside him.

"By the time my vacation is finished, I'll figure something out," he finally said.

"I just want what's best for Joey," she replied. "I don't want him getting too attached to me, since I have no intention of being in his life long-term."

Her words shot new tiny little daggers through his heart. If she didn't intend to be in Joey's life long-term, then she definitely had no intention to be in Tony's life.

"That's what I want, too," he agreed. *You'll never amount to anything. You're nothing but a dirty half-breed and nobody will ever love you.* The deep, familiar voice slammed into his brain.

"Then I guess I'll see you this evening after dinner," he said.

"Good, you know Joey loves spending time with you."

He gave her a curt nod, clutched the papers from Halena more tightly in his fist and then turned to head to the cowboy motel in the distance.

Chapter 12

Cassie had insisted on a special night. After a week of eating Halena's food and them all being cooped up in the house, she'd decided it would be fun to go down to the cowboy dining room for dinner that evening.

Mary and Joey were ready and seated on the sofa waiting for Halena and Cassie. The last few days had been difficult ones. After her talk with Tony about needing him to make other arrangements for Joey when his vacation was finished, the air between them had been fraught with an uncomfortable tension she didn't quite understand.

Surely, he hadn't expected their arrangement to last forever and she'd made it clear to him that she wasn't interested in a romantic relationship with him. He shouldn't have been surprised that she'd finally put a time limit on things.

And yet his eyes now held a faint wounded look when he gazed at her. Their conversations since then had been stilted and mostly revolved around all things Joey.

That man is head over heels in love with you.

Cassie's words had played and replayed in Mary's mind. One minute she rejected the very idea. She told herself Tony needed her but he certainly wasn't in love with her.

Then the next minute her heart ached for both Tony and herself because she saw his love flooding out of his eyes, she felt his love for her in his simplest touch.

But in the end, it didn't matter whether he loved her or not. Their future was written in stone and it wasn't one that ended with the two of them together with a happily-ever-after.

Cassie came down the stairs, looking gorgeous in a pair of designer jeans and a pink Western shirt with pearl buttons. "I had Cookie do a barbecue night for dinner," she said. "You're all in for a real treat. Nobody does pulled pork and baked beans like Cookie."

"Sounds good to me," Mary replied.

"And after dinner we have to hang around long enough for you to hear Mac sing and play his guitar. He has a wonderful voice." Cassie smiled. "And Clay will entertain you with stories of his womanizing, which aren't true, and Brody will brood because that's what he does…"

"How are you ever going to leave here?" Mary asked. "You obviously have a lot of affection for all the men."

Cassie sighed. "Why do you think I'm still here? These men were like my aunt's sons and this is the only home they've known for most of their lives. When I first arrived here, my thought was to sell the place immediately and then the skeletons were found and I couldn't sell. Now I'm just so torn between the life I thought I wanted and this place that my aunt loved so much."

"I don't envy you that kind of decision," Mary said.

"I've already planned for a big barn dance at the end of October. I figure if I'm going to make a move, right after that would be the time, hopefully before the first snow flies."

"Tony has told me that the men think a lot of you."

"Are you trying to make my final decision more difficult on me?" Cassie asked with a wry grin. "I had a dream for myself for years and sometimes it's hard to let go of dreams."

"Trust me, I know," Mary replied.

The conversation was halted when Halena came down the stairs. Mary was surprised that she wore a pair of jeans and a T-shirt advertising Mary's business. Her hair was neatly braided and she looked almost normal, if one didn't look too closely at the wicked gleam in her eyes.

"A whole room of handsome cowboys," she exclaimed. "I can't wait!"

"No pinching, Grandmother," Mary warned her.

"I have no idea what you're talking about," Halena replied with her dark eyes wide with innocence.

"Tony should be here anytime to escort us," Cassie said and as if on cue Tony and Clay came through the back door.

"Are we ready for some barbecue?" Tony asked.

"Personally, I'm starving," Mary replied.

Clay grinned. "It's not every day I get to escort three beautiful women to dinner."

"Down, boy," Halena replied, making them all laugh. She grabbed the bouncy chair and minutes later they all made their way across the lawn and down a slight hill to the cowboy motel.

Both Tony and Clay had their guns in their hands, a grim reminder that, although the past week had been peaceful, Ash Moreland was still at large.

As they walked, Halena grilled Tony on Choctaw history and he passed each question with flying colors, having obviously really studied the papers she'd printed for him.

"I'm glad you passed," Halena said. "I would've really hated to give up my pink hat."

"And I really don't want to wear it," Tony retorted.

Before they even reached the back of the building, the savory scent of barbecue wafted in the air. "Smell that, Joey?" Mary said to the little boy in her arms. "Someday maybe you'll be a cowboy and eat pulled pork." He laughed and wiggled as if the very idea excited him.

When they got inside the large dining area, Tony took Joey from her and placed him in his bouncy seat and then set the seat in the center of one of the wooden tables.

They were greeted with friendliness by the other men. Throughout the week Mary had managed to put names with faces for all the ranch hands.

Several of the men beelined straight for the baby. Mary watched in amusement as Flint and Sawyer made goofy faces to Joey's delight. There was something magical about watching grown men act like fools just to hear a baby's laughter.

"The men waited for us to arrive so you women could go through the food line first," Tony said.

"Then let's go," Halena replied.

The food was served buffet-style. There were thick rolls for the pulled pork, baked beans, coleslaw and potato salad. Dessert was either cherry or apple cobbler.

Cookie stood at the end of the table, his arms crossed and a frown on his face. He might not look friendly, but it was obvious he knew how to cook.

They filled their plates and then sat at the long picnic table, where Joey served as the centerpiece. The men were all respectful and Mary suspected they were on their best behavior, since their boss was in the house.

Once all of them had filled their plates and were seated at the tables, conversation and laughter filled the room. The food was excellent and Joey cooed and blew spit bubbles for anyone who paid attention to him.

Halena got a second helping of the cherry cobbler, and when she returned to the table, her gaze remained on Cookie. "Does he always look like he's got a stick up his—"

"Grandmother," Mary said sharply, cutting off Halena's sentence.

Tony laughed. "Yeah, pretty much. I'm not sure I've seen him smile more than once or twice in the last fifteen years, but there's no question that the man can cook."

It was difficult to think about anything bad with the warmth of the company surrounding her and the obvious camaraderie in the room.

After they finished eating, some of the men moved from the tables to a recreational area, while others drifted back outside to finish up evening chores.

"Come on," Clay said. "We've saved you beautiful ladies the seat of honor on the sofa."

Tony grabbed Joey's seat and they all got comfortable on the oversize sofa while Mac McBride pulled out his guitar and began to entertain them.

He played old standards and they all sang along. Even Halena sang loudly despite the fact that she couldn't carry a tune if her life depended on it.

The music and the laughter created a warm bubble around Mary. She couldn't imagine how Cassie could ever leave all this behind.

It wasn't long before Halena stood. "I think it's time for me to say good-night," she said.

Cassie got up as well. "Me, too." She looked at Mary. "But you stay and enjoy more of the fun. I'll take Joey and give him a bottle and tuck him into bed."

"Oh, no," Mary protested.

"Please, Mary…stay," Tony said softly.

"I'm sure between Cassie and me we can wrestle the little warrior into bed," Halena said. "Relax for a while, Mary. Enjoy the rest of the evening."

"I'll walk you ladies back up to the house." Sawyer stood from a folding chair where he'd been seated.

Mary watched as they left the building, feeling as if she should have gone with them, but not wanting to end the night of fun. Right now there were no concerns banging around in her head. She was just in the moment with the music and the men and the odd feeling of belonging.

Tony joined her on the sofa, his nearness as familiar to her as the beat of her own heart. Mac continued to play, this time slower songs, and when he lent his voice to the guitar, it was sheer magic.

Mary was shocked when she glanced at a clock on the wall and saw that it was just after ten. "I should go," she said when there was a break in the music.

"And I'm done for tonight," Mac said. He smiled at Mary. "It was nice having all of you here tonight, Mary."

"Thanks, Mac. I appreciated being able to enjoy the entertainment. You're so talented."

"I'm just a cowboy who likes to strum his guitar and sing," he replied.

"I'll walk you back to the house," Tony said.

Goodbyes were said all around and Tony and Mary left the dining room with several of the other men trailing behind them. "I need to stop in my room and grab a jacket," Tony said. "I'm on night guard duty tonight and it gets cool before morning."

Mary followed him to his room, and when he opened the door, she peeked in with interest. She was vaguely surprised that there wasn't much to see. It was a sterile, impersonal environment for a man who had lived in the space for fifteen years.

"Maybe we could take some pictures of Joey and you could hang them on a wall," she suggested.

"That would be nice." He grabbed a denim jacket from the closet and then stepped back outside and closed the door. Together they started across the expanse of lawn toward the big house.

"What a nice night it's been," she said. It had been wonderful to cut loose just a bit and put the worries and the danger behind for a little while. The moon overhead was full, shining down a beautiful silvery light that illuminated their way.

"It was fun," Tony agreed. His hand was on the butt of his gun and he gazed around the landscape as they walked.

Just that quickly, an edge of nervous tension returned to her. Was Ash Moreland out here right now? Hiding behind a tree? Maybe in the hayloft of the barn?

Was he watching them right this minute? Was he watching and waiting? She moved closer to Tony's side.

"I thought maybe tomorrow I'd take you to the house so you can see all the repairs finished," he said.

"That would be nice. I can't believe how quickly Frankie got it all done."

"He's definitely good at what he does and I was lucky to catch him when he had no other jobs pending."

As they got close enough to the house, Sawyer saw them in the yard light and began to walk toward them. "All is quiet on the home front," he said when he reached them. "You're on night duty?"

"That's right," Tony replied.

"Then I'll see you sometime tomorrow. Good night, Mary."

"Good night, Sawyer, and thanks."

He gave an easy wave of his hand and then headed back to the cowboy motel. Tony and Mary arrived at the back porch. "Mary, sit with me for just a few more minutes," he said and gestured to the two lawn chairs on the porch.

She hesitated, her desire to spend a little time with him battling with what she knew she should do. "Okay," she finally said. "But just for a bit." She eased down into one of the chairs and he sat next to her.

For the next few minutes they talked about the cowboys they'd had dinner with, the food they had eaten and the music that had filled the dining room.

"It would be a shame if Cassie sold this place," she said. "There's such a feeling of brotherhood between all of you."

He looked out toward the cowboy motel. "We've been together for fifteen years. Each morning we all get up and wonder if Cassie will decide to sell and we'll all not only lose our jobs, but also our home."

He twisted his chair to face hers. "But in the last three weeks I've realized that this place is my childhood home. It's time for me to find my grown-up home and I believe I've found that with you."

Her heart stopped, leaving her not just breathless but unable to speak. *No, don't go there*, a voice in her head cried. *Don't say anything more, Tony. Please don't do this.*

He got up from his chair and pulled her to her feet

and before she knew it, before she could protest, he was kissing her, and God help her, but she was kissing him back.

Last kiss, she told herself. This was the very last kiss she would ever share with him. This was the very last time she'd be held in his arms. She kissed him with all the passion she had inside her. She hoped to kiss him in a way that he would never forget her.

"I love you, Mary," he said when the kiss finally ended. He took two steps back from her. "I didn't think I knew how to love, I didn't believe it was possible for me, but I love you and I want to spend the rest of my life with you."

He spoke quickly, as if he couldn't get the words out fast enough. She could only stare at him in horror, wishing he'd stop.

"For years I didn't think I was worthy of love, but my time with you and Halena and caring for Joey has made me realize I deserve this. I love you, Mary, and I know we all could have a wonderful future together."

He stopped talking with his mouth, but his intense, tender gaze continued to speak to her of love. Her heart began to beat again, a slow rhythm of dread and of bitter regret.

She should have never kissed him. She definitely shouldn't have kissed him like she meant it. She should have never slept with him. It had given him hope where there was none. She should have maintained a strictly professional relationship with him, one that didn't include long, intimate talks and laughter.

"Mary, please say something."

She wanted to escape. She wanted to weep because she was in love with him, but it was a love she would deny both of them, knowing that in the end he would run from the woman she could never be.

"Tony." Her mouth was unaccountably dry even as she felt the hot moisture that tried to fill her eyes. "This has been a crazy ride that we've been on. With me helping you care for Joey I can understand why you think you might love me."

He leaned forward. "I don't think anything. This has nothing to do with Joey, this is about the way I feel about you and I know what's in my heart."

"But it isn't in my heart," she replied softly. Her heart broke even as she knew she was breaking his.

He appeared stricken. He stared at her for a long moment and then sat back in the chair. His eyes flared and then narrowed. "I don't believe you," he said flatly.

She half turned toward the back door. Escape. She needed to escape before he somehow convinced her that love would be enough to sustain them, that somehow, some way, they could have a future together.

"Tony, it doesn't matter whether you believe me or not. I know what's in my heart and I'm sorry, but I'm not in love with you."

She didn't say good-night and she didn't give him another chance to speak. She ran for the back door, needing to get inside before the tears that pressed hot and heavy began to fall.

She didn't love him.

He'd made a fool of himself. Hell, he was a fool to

really believe a beautiful, wonderful woman like Mary could ever love a man like him. But he'd been so certain of her feelings.

He could have sworn he'd seen love shining in her eyes when she gazed at him. He had been so certain that he'd tasted her love for him on her lips when they'd kissed.

The kiss they'd just shared still burned his lips. She'd clung to him, had kissed his with a passion that couldn't have been a lie. Still…she'd said she didn't love him.

He sank down in the chair, his heart pressing so tightly against his ribs he could scarcely draw a breath. Even now he could smell the scent of her, the spicy fragrance he'd come to identify as love.

Tears misted his vision as a wealth of loss swept through him. How could he hurt so badly about something he'd never had? He stared up at the full moon. It was weeping and the stars spun crazily in the sky.

He remembered Halena's dream walk. He was in her dream and the sky had gone mad…the moon wept and the stars spun. He swiped at his tears and cursed himself for being weak and stupid.

But wasn't that what Hank had always told him? That he was weak and stupid and would never amount to anything? He was a half-breed who had no place in the world.

"No." The single word of protest escaped his lips. No, he wasn't that little boy who Hank and his family had tormented.

In the last week Tony had learned the pride of his

people. He'd embraced all of who and what he was, and it was nothing like Hank had said.

Tony was the sum of all things good from his Choctaw heritage and his white blood. He was so much more than a half-breed. He was a man of strength and determination. He was a good man who loved Joey and a man who wasn't giving up so easily on Mary.

In the past seven days he'd looked back on his past. He'd never understand why his mother had given him to Hank and Betty Ryan to raise, but he'd made peace with that part of his life. He had survived. He was a survivor and his past no longer dictated who he was.

The man who had always lived in the moment, who had never looked back and never looked forward, was gone. Tony now looked toward the future with hope and anticipation.

He frowned and ran a hand over his mouth. The kiss he'd shared with Mary still lingered on his lips and her eyes had spoken of love even as her mouth had denied it. No, he definitely wasn't going to go quietly into the night where Mary was concerned.

He could have sworn that just before she'd run inside what he'd seen in her eyes was fear. Of course, she was afraid with Ash Moreland still a threat. With everything that had happened and with the potential of something else bad happening she was certainly afraid. How could she see a future with him when there was so much danger in the air around him?

He could be a patient man. Eventually Ash would no longer be a threat and life would return to normal. Maybe then she could fully embrace her love for him.

The leaves on the trees whispered to him that Mary loved him.

A cool breeze whipped around him and he reached for his coat and shrugged it on. Tonight he would stand guard to protect them all and tomorrow he would continue to love Mary.

He settled back in the chair and waited for the night to pass.

Chief of police Dillon Bowie stood at his window in his office and stared out to the dark streets of the town he loved. It was late. He should be home in bed, but since the discovery of the seven skeletons on the Holiday ranch, what little sleep he got each night was haunted and tormented by souls not at rest.

And as if those murders weren't enough to keep him tossing and turning, he now had a murderous drug lord to contend with in his town. He'd passed around pictures of Ash to all of his officers, but so far nobody had seen the man.

As long as Amy's baby was here in Bitterroot, Dillon knew there was a real and present danger in town. He rubbed the center of his forehead, where a headache had pounded for the last couple of hours. There had already been an attempted kidnapping and a fire—he worried about what came next.

He returned to his desk and slumped down in his chair. He'd been in close touch with the Oklahoma City authorities about Ash Moreland and Amy's murder. So far there wasn't enough evidence to make an arrest in the case, and they couldn't make an arrest if they couldn't find the man.

His biggest concern was that they couldn't find him because he wasn't in Oklahoma City any longer. He was someplace here in Bitterroot...but where?

With a weary sigh he opened his desk drawer and pulled out a bottle of aspirin that was nestled against a bottle of antacid tablets. The two bottles had been his best friends lately. He shook two of the painkillers into his hand and then chased them down with a sip of cold coffee.

He leaned his head back, closed his eyes and once again thought of those seven skeletons. Two of them had now been identified, both runaways who had somehow wound up murdered and buried on the Holiday ranch.

Other than the identifications being made, there were no other leads for him to follow, no clues forthcoming after all these years. It was basically a cold case and Dillon feared that it would remain a cold case forever unless he could somehow solve it.

He opened his eyes and pulled open a second desk drawer. A small plastic evidence bag displayed a man's gold ring with a black onyx stone. The ring had been found at the bottom of the burial site and Dillon knew in his gut it belonged to the murderer.

He also believed that the man who had committed these murders was still working on the Holiday ranch. Unfortunately, the ring wasn't like Cinderella's slipper. The men had been boys when they'd arrived at the ranch. The shape and size of their fingers had changed in the years that had passed.

He had no idea which of them had worn that ring, which finger it had slipped off when the murderer had buried the bodies one on top of the other. But Dillon knew with a burning instinct that one of the Holiday cowboys was a murderer. He just had no idea which one.

Chapter 13

It was a gray, cloudy day that greeted Mary when she awakened the next morning. Joey was still asleep in the crib when she crept to the window and peered outside.

It looked like rain and that was only fitting. Every loss she had ever suffered was accompanied by rain and this morning the loss that resounded in her heart was worthy of a hurricane.

She wished Tony had never told her he loved her. She desperately wished she could unhear his words, unsee his eyes as he'd bared his soul to her.

She'd broken his heart and she hated herself for that. She was culpable in the mess that this had become. She'd kissed him and she'd made love with him. She'd reveled in the love she had for him, in the love he'd shown her, even knowing that there was no future for the two of them.

It had been wrong and it had been unfair to him. He was such a good man, a man who had finally come into his own just in time for her to break his heart.

She had no idea what to expect today. Did he now hate her? Would he insist she leave here and have nothing to do with Joey anymore?

She gazed down at the sleeping boy. The breasts she no longer had ached and the womb that had been taken from her cried with emptiness.

Tony was meant to be a father. She'd seen how he loved, how he protected a baby he wasn't even sure was his. He would eventually find love with a real woman who could give him more babies, a woman who could nurse his babies.

She grabbed her clothes and went into the bathroom for a quick shower. Numb. She felt utterly drained and numb. *You fool, what did you expect from all of this?* a little voice derided her as the hot water pelted her.

In your foolish mind did you really believe that somehow Joey could be your baby and Tony could be your man? Did you really think there was a happy ending for you here?

Tony's words of love thundered in her brain as she dried off, dressed and then braided her wet hair down her back. By the time she returned to the bedroom Joey was awake and demanding his breakfast.

Stay numb, she told herself. Don't think. It was the only way she thought she could get through the day. She carried Joey down the stairs to the kitchen, where

Halena and Cassie were seated at the table drinking coffee. Joey flashed them a quick smile and then his features screwed up for a wail.

"Somebody is definitely hungry," Cassie said.

"He's a demanding little cuss when he's hungry," Halena replied.

Mary grabbed a bottle and within minutes Joey was happily drinking his breakfast and Cassie had poured Mary a cup of coffee.

"Did you have fun last night?" Cassie asked her.

"It was very nice," she replied. "Mac is certainly talented."

"I burped barbecue all night," Halena exclaimed. "But it was worth it. That pulled pork was delicious."

As the two women talked about barbecue and their favorite country and western songs, Mary sipped her coffee and tried to pretend that everything was fine, that her heart wasn't shredded and bleeding.

She managed to get through breakfast and made small talk. They had just finished eating when Adam came in to speak with Cassie about ranch business. They excused themselves and went into the small formal parlor to talk.

"I see a darkness in you this morning," Halena said when they were alone.

Mary turned to look out the window as a light rain began to fall. "You know how much I hate rainy days."

"We need rainy days so we can fully enjoy the sun when it shines again. Besides, rain is important for life."

"I think we should move to Arizona, where it almost never rains."

"And I think you're out of sorts because you know it won't be long before you say goodbye to Joey."

Mary looked at her grandmother. "Maybe that's it," she said. Just as well that Halena believed that was the reason for Mary's mood. "Actually, I don't feel very well today. Maybe you could watch Joey until Tony arrives and I'll go back to bed."

Halena gazed at her intently and Mary fought the childish impulse to squirm beneath her scrutiny. "Please, Grandmother," she said softly.

Halena nodded and Mary escaped. She raced up the stairs to her bedroom and threw herself on the bed. Rain began to pitter-patter against the windowpane and Mary fought against the tears she hadn't shed the night before.

Before this moment she hadn't been able to see how this all would end, but now she saw the ending in stark and painful detail. Of course the ending was that she'd be alone. She'd come to peace with being alone when Rick had walked out on her, but she realized now that she'd been entertaining the fantasy of a different ending this time.

The rain came down in torrents, as did her tears, and she cried until she was so exhausted she fell asleep. She awakened to the sound of laughter drifting up the stairs. A glance at the clock let her know it was lunchtime.

She went into the bathroom and sluiced cold water over her face, hoping that her earlier tears didn't show on her face, and then she headed downstairs.

As she heard Tony's familiar deep voice, she steeled herself for seeing him again after the night before. "Ah, Sleeping Beauty has awakened," Cassie said as Mary walked into the kitchen. Cassie stood at the stove and stirred something in a large pot.

"Halena said you weren't feeling well. Are you feeling better now?" Tony's features radiated nothing but genuine concern.

Her heart squeezed tight. She would have been more comfortable if he'd been cold or indifferent to her, but his caring cut her to her very core.

"Yes, I'm feeling better," she replied.

"You're just in time for a nice bowl of vegetable soup," Cassie said. "And I know you'll like it because it's your grandmother's recipe."

"It's definitely a soup kind of day," Halena said.

Mary glanced out the window, where gray clouds still hung low and heavy. Joey, who was in his bouncy chair on the floor, gurgled loudly, as if attempting to get her attention.

She leaned down to him. "What are you doing, Joey? Have you been entertaining everyone while I've been lazing around in bed?" He squealed with excitement, kicked his sturdy legs and gnawed on the back of his fist.

"He's teething," Halena said. "I think maybe he's going to sprout a little chopper any day now."

Mary looked at her in surprise. "A tooth?" She glanced at Tony and then quickly averted her gaze back to Joey. As crazy as it sounded, it felt like a milestone she and Tony had shared together. A baby's first tooth.

She wouldn't be around to see any of his other milestones. She wouldn't hear Joey say his first word or take his first step. She wouldn't cry just a little bit as she put him on a big yellow bus for his first day of school.

She shoved the depressing thought aside. "Cassie, is there anything I can help you with?" She needed to do something, anything, besides sit at this table across from Tony.

"Sure, you could get down bowls and plates and then grab the crackers in the pantry," Cassie replied.

She felt Tony's gaze on her as she reached to take down bowls and plates from the cabinet. His eyes tracked her as she walked across the room to the walk-in pantry.

She felt no recriminations from him, no negative energy at all. It was as if last night had never happened. If that was the way he wanted it, she was more than happy to play it that way.

Lunch was actually pleasant. Adam joined them and the talk centered around the ranch and the rain. The soup was delicious and her nerves faded away with the very normalcy of her conversation with Tony and the others.

She couldn't help but notice how solicitous Adam was of Cassie and how often his gaze lingered on her. Mary wondered if Cassie had any idea that Adam had feelings for her. She thought about saying something to Cassie about it but decided she had no business meddling in anyone else's relationship, since she'd so badly botched hers with Tony.

Adam left after lunch and after the dishes were put away Cassie brought out the game of Monopoly. "I read in my Aunt Cass's diary that she and my uncle often played this on rainy days, so who is game?"

"Don't let Grandmother be banker," Mary said. "She cheats."

"My granddaughter speaks with forked tongue," Halena replied, causing everyone to laugh.

Tony was designated banker and it didn't take long to see they were all highly competitive. The dice rolled fast and money changed hands as properties were bought and rent was collected.

Joey napped while the game continued, the stakes getting higher and the laughter more rowdy. It was almost dinnertime when they finally conceded that Halena was the winner with the most money and property.

They ate more soup for supper and after that both Halena and Cassie went upstairs to their rooms, leaving Tony and Mary in the great room with Joey on the floor. It was then that her nerves jumped back to life.

She tensed as Tony sank down next to her on the sofa. "Relax, Mary," he said. "I don't want my nearness to you to stress you out."

"I don't know how to act with you," she confessed.

"Act like Mary," he replied. "Act like the intelligent, beautiful, funny woman that you are. We're good, Mary, and there's nothing for you to worry about."

Why did he have to be so wonderful? Why couldn't he be a jackass? She gazed down at Joey, who was happily entertaining himself with his fist in his mouth and his foot in his other hand.

"What are you going to do, Tony?" She looked back up at him. He had to know that after their conversation last night she wasn't a viable part of his or Joey's future.

He frowned thoughtfully. "I've been working all

kinds of potential answers to that question around in my head." He leaned back against the cushion and released a deep sigh.

"If Ash isn't caught in the next couple of days, then I'm going to get an apartment or a house in town. I've got enough money stashed away that I can be a stay-at-home dad for a year or so."

"You'd do that?"

"I'll do whatever it takes," he replied firmly. "I'm sure he's out there, Mary. What I'm hoping is that he'll see where I go and he won't bother you or your grandmother ever again. He's after Joey. There's no reason to think that you will be in danger anymore."

"Does Cassie know your plan?"

"Not yet. I'm hoping to get a chance to talk to her first thing tomorrow, and then if you don't mind keeping an eye on Joey for a couple of hours, I'm planning on heading into town to see if I can find a place to live."

Mary sighed and gazed down at Joey. He was such a little bundle of joy to be at the heart of such upheaval. "You're writing wonderful things in his book of life, Tony."

"I'd hoped that you'd be around to add a couple of chapters to that book."

His voice was so soft, so tender, and she refused to look up and meet his eyes. "You know I'll be more than happy to watch Joey for however long you need tomorrow," she replied.

Joey began to fuss. It was time for his fill-up bottle before bedtime. Mary rose and picked up Joey. "Tony, why don't you go ahead and go. I know you were on guard duty last night and you were here pretty early this morning. You've got to be exhausted. I'll just give him his bottle and put him to bed."

"I am tired," he admitted.

Together they walked from the living room to the kitchen. Tony kissed Joey on the forehead, his nearness threatening to weaken her knees. He raised his head and held her gaze for a long moment.

"I'm not giving up on us, Mary." He turned and went out the back door.

She remained standing still, her heart pounding. It was only when Joey began to cry in earnest that she hurried for his bottle.

She carried the baby back into the great room and sank down on the sofa to feed him. As Joey greedily chugged his meal, Tony's parting words went around and around in her head.

I'm not giving up on us.

So, he intended to make this difficult for her. What he didn't understand was that it took two to tango…and she wasn't dancing.

Tony looked around the small apartment with a frown. Although it had been advertised as a two-bedroom, one of the bedrooms was no bigger than a walk-in closet.

He didn't want Joey staying in a closet. He turned to the landlord, Bernie Davies, with a smile. "Thanks for showing it to me, Bernie. I've got a couple of other options to check out, but one way or the other I'll get back in touch with you."

"You'd better make up your mind fast," Bernie replied

as the two men walked out of the place. "Empty apartments don't last long in a town where there's only one small apartment complex."

The Bitterroot apartment complex had a grand total of eight units and as Tony drove away he hoped to find something better for him and Joey.

Of course, the ideal situation would be Mary's house. He could easily imagine the spare room being Joey's bedroom. His crib would be in front of the window, where he could see the morning sun come up, and Mary would make a special dream catcher to hang over his head.

Tony could also easily fantasize being in Mary's bed each night, her warm body curled into his after they'd made love. They could all be such a happy family.

Last night when he'd told Mary what he intended to do, he'd hoped she would fall into his arms and profess her love for him. He'd so desperately wanted her to tell him he didn't need to look for any other place to live, that his home would be with her.

He'd been convinced that he just needed to fight harder for her and allow her whatever time she needed to come to the conclusion they belonged together. However, she'd been distant that morning and his hope for a future with her was slowly slipping away.

He drove down Main Street and arrived at the address of a rental house. It was an old two-story newly painted gray with black trim.

The owner, Amanda Sanders, stood on the wraparound front porch and greeted him with a wide smile as he got out of his truck and approached her.

"Afternoon, Tony," she said.

"Same to you." He walked up on the porch and took a look around at the yard. The lawn was neat with only a small pile of autumn leaves around the base of an oak tree.

"Shall we go inside so you can have a look around?" Amanda asked.

"Absolutely," Tony agreed. He followed the old woman into a small foyer. He knew Amanda was a widow and probably depended on the rent of this house to supplement her finances.

Hardwood floors gleamed as they walked into a nice-sized living room with a staircase leading to the up-stairs. The walls also appeared newly painted. "How long has it been empty?" he asked.

"About a month. The last tenants had no respect for property. They left me a real mess here, but as you can see it's in tip-top shape now."

The kitchen was adequate and the upstairs bedrooms were roomy. There was plenty of closet space and the bathrooms boasted new fixtures.

The house was nice. The backyard was big and the rent was reasonable. There was absolutely nothing to stop him from writing a check and claiming the place as his new home. Except it didn't feel like home.

Home was a place where Halena wore mismatched clothes and sometimes a hat. It was where Mary wove baskets and action movies played on the television and the leaves on the trees whispered that love and happiness would last forever.

"So, what do you think?" Amanda asked.

Tony jammed his hands in his pockets. "I'll give you a call later this evening and let you know what I've decided. I've still got a couple of other places to check out."

That was a lie. He hadn't seen anything else in the paper that would be viable except the apartment and Amanda's place, and out of the two, this was really perfect. But he was reluctant to commit himself.

Minutes later as he headed back to the ranch he kicked himself for being a fool. He believed Mary was in love with him, but something held her back, but that might just be a fool's thought.

He had no choice but to build a life without her. So, why hadn't he written a deposit check to Amanda? Why hadn't he taken the first step in securing a safe place for Joey?

By the time he reached the ranch he was in a foul mood. Instead of taking his mood to the big house, he decided to take a quick horseback ride. It had been too long since he'd taken Rascal out for some exercise.

Brody was in the stables when Tony walked in. "You taking Rascal out?"

"Yeah, I figured I could take a short ride before dinner," Tony replied.

"Do you mind some company? I need to get Midnight out for a ride."

Tony looked at Brody in surprise. "Wouldn't mind the company at all."

The two men got busy saddling up. Tony was surprised by Brody riding with him. Brody rarely actively sought the company of the others.

Brody was the man you wanted next to you in a fight, but he was also the man Tony knew the least about even after living with him for the past fifteen years.

They mounted and left the stable at a walking pace, heading for the pasture in the distance. "I heard you talked to Cassie this morning about quitting and moving into town," Brody said.

Tony shook his head with a wry grin. "No secrets on this ranch."

"Except maybe one." Brody gazed to the right as they passed the burial pit where the skeletons had been found.

Tony's stomach muscles tightened. "I think Dillon is barking up the wrong tree thinking any of us might be responsible for that."

"I don't know what I think about it. Now, let's ride." Brody nudged his horse with his heels and took off.

Tony followed, allowing Rascal full rein to run like the wind. The air smelled of wood smoke and cattle, of dying leaves and a hint of pumpkin.

September had turned to October. It was hard to believe that it had been a month ago that he'd appeared on Mary's doorstep with Joey.

He shoved all thoughts out of his mind and just focused on the wind on his face, the familiar smells of the ranch that had always comforted him.

They raced across the pasture until they reached a stand of trees and a dry creek bed. Only then did they rein in and return to a slower pace.

"You're going to miss us," Brody said.

"I will," Tony replied.

"What if Joey isn't yours?"

"Then I'll adopt him." Funny, Tony had never really considered what he'd do if the DNA test came back and he discovered he wasn't Joey's biological father and yet his answer to Brody had come easily.

"Amy is dead, and if justice is served, Ash Moreland will spend the rest of his life behind bars," he continued. The last thing he wanted was for Joey to go into foster care.

He sat up straighter in his saddle as a new thought blossomed in his head. Was the reason Mary refused to admit she loved him because she couldn't have children? Did she just assume that eventually he'd want more kids and therefore she couldn't be right for him?

"Brody, I'm heading back," Tony said. He couldn't wait to get to the big house and tell Mary that her inability to bear a child didn't matter to him.

A new hope shimmered in his heart as he raced Rascal back to the stable. He unsaddled and stalled the horse in record time and then hurried to the back door.

Cassie greeted him. She and Halena were bustling in the kitchen and cooking dinner. Mary sat at the table with Joey in his bouncy chair.

"Don't get in their way," Mary said. "I offered to help and they practically banished me to my room."

The lightness of her tone pleased him, as did the beautiful vision she presented clad in jeans and a pink T-shirt and with her hair loose around her shoulders. Her features were relaxed and a smile curved her lips.

"We're attempting to create culinary magic in here," Cassie said.

"Far be it for me to interfere with magic," Tony replied. "Mary, would you mind talking to me outside for a minute?"

He hated the wariness that suddenly leaped into her eyes.

"Go on, I'll keep an eye on Joey," Halena said.

She got up and followed him out to the back porch. "Did you find a place to rent today?" she asked.

"I found a house that I'm considering. Mary, a few minutes ago I was taking a quick horse ride with Brody and he asked me what I was going to do if the DNA results showed that I wasn't the father. I told him if that was the case, then I'd adopt Joey."

"That would be wonderful, Tony." She visibly relaxed once again.

"What would be even more wonderful is if you'd marry me and we can adopt more babies if we decide we want to give Joey brothers or sisters."

For just a moment her eyes shone with sweet yearning, with a wistfulness that nearly took his breath away as his heart swelled full in his chest. But just as quickly as the emotions had come, they vanished and her gaze became dark and unfathomable.

"You have to stop," she said and took a step back from him. "You have to stop this, Tony." Her lower lip began to tremble. "We don't have a future together. We're not going to get married and adopt children. Find a nice woman who makes you happy."

"I already have," he replied. Again he was half-breathless, this time as his heart deflated and disappeared into a cold emptiness. "Mary, I won't stop believing that you love me. I just wish you'd tell me what's holding you back."

She straightened her shoulders and lifted her chin. "I don't owe you any explanation. I'm telling you that you have no future with me and that's enough said."

He stared at her, loving her even as he saw nothing but rejection in her eyes. He released a hollow sigh and jammed his hands into his pockets. "It doesn't matter to me that you can't have children. I'm sure there are Native American babies who need the good and loving home that you and I could provide. Maybe there's a little boy like I was who doesn't know where he fits in the world."

A shaft of pain crossed her features. "I'm finished with this discussion." She turned to go back into the house and even though Tony wanted to stop her…he let her go.

He pulled his hands from his pockets and set off across the lawn toward the cowboy dining room, where dinner would be served soon. He had no appetite. His stomach was filled with a huge stone of misery.

He'd been so sure that her inability to have a child was what had held her back. He'd also been certain that if he told her he didn't care about it, then she'd fall into his arms.

As he trudged across the huge yard, he made a vow that first thing in the morning he would call Amanda and secure the house for his future. Tomorrow he would focus on his role as a single father and what needed to be done to assure Joey had a good home. He'd need to buy furniture and make sure all the utilities were turned on. He'd give Joey a nursery fit for a king. Starting to-morrow he was not going to think about Mary and what might have been.

In the meantime all he had to do was get through this long and lonely night.

Chapter 14

Amy's body had been released to Tony. There had been nobody else to claim her and the last thing he had wanted was for her to remain any longer in the morgue.

Cassie had been gracious enough to allow her to be buried in the Holiday ranch cemetery. Tony had spoken to Reverend Wally Donaldson, who had agreed to officiate for a small funeral.

It had been two days since Tony had once again confessed his love for Mary and although they had been friendly with each other he'd also sensed that she was cautious around him. She'd made sure that in those two days they had never been alone in a room.

He now pulled on a black suit jacket, which Cass had insisted all the men have for funerals and weddings, and headed for the house.

As he walked, he glanced over to the cemetery where Amy's casket was already in place. Today he would bury the mother of his child. It hadn't seemed real until this moment.

He should have bought flowers. Somebody should have thought of flowers. The casket looked so bare, so lonely just sitting there next to the pit that had been dug to receive it.

It had all happened so fast. Dillon had told them that there was nobody to claim Amy's body. She had no family and there hadn't been any other friends. The arrangements had been fast so she could be laid to rest as quickly as possible.

He snapped his head forward and gave a sober smile to Clay, who stood just outside the back door of the house. "At least the sun is shining," Clay offered.

"Yeah, it's a beautiful day," Tony agreed. Once again he looked toward the cemetery. "It somehow seems fitting that she'd wind up here. Cass was so good about taking in troubled souls."

Clay's blue eyes darkened. "I still miss her."

"Yeah, me, too," Tony admitted. He laughed suddenly. "All I have to say is that Amy better not misbehave in Heaven. Cass will twist her ears back, snap that bullwhip of hers and scare the daylights out of Amy."

Clay chuckled. "You've got that right."

Tony checked his wristwatch. They had set the time of the funeral for noon and afterward Cookie would have a meal for everyone in the cowboy dining room. It was now just a little after eleven thirty.

"Here come the rest of the men," Clay said.

Tony turned around to see the rest of the cowboys heading up the hill. They looked like a band of brothers clad in their black suit jackets and blue jeans, and a lump rose in the back of Tony's throat.

He hadn't asked any of them to attend the funeral. He hadn't expected any of them to come. But here they were, lending their support and prayers for a woman most of them hadn't even personally known.

Each of them greeted Tony with a clap on the back and somber smiles. "I didn't expect you all to be here," he said around the lump in his throat.

"Why wouldn't we be?" Adam replied. "When one of us hurts, all of us hurt."

They turned at the sound of gravel crunching under car tires. Reverend Donaldson's red compact car pulled down the driveway and parked.

The old man got out of the car, his silver hair shining in the late-morning sunshine. He carried a small Bible and greeted Tony with a soft smile.

"Thank you for coming on such short notice, Reverend," Tony said and shook his hand.

He looked around at all the other men. "It seems the only time I see most of you is either at weddings or at funerals," he chided gently. "It would be nice to see you occasionally in church on Sunday mornings."

The men coughed, scuffed their feet on the ground and mumbled excuses about Sundays and church and ranch work. Tony might have laughed if at that moment the back door hadn't opened and the women came outside.

Tony drank in the sight of Mary holding a sleeping

Joey. She was dressed in dark slacks, a white blouse and a lightweight black jacket. Joey was nestled against her chest in a warm sleeper and his blue blanket.

Cassie was also dressed appropriately for the somber occasion. Halena was dressed for a party in a bright red beaded skirt, an orange-and-red flowered blouse and red sparkly earrings dangling down to her shoulders.

"The rest of you can wear your mourning black and be sad, but as far as I'm concerned it's a day of celebration. Amy is going home with the Lord," she exclaimed.

"Amen," Reverend Donaldson replied. "Are we expecting anyone else to come?"

Sadness swept through Tony at the fact that Amy would be mourned by two women from her childhood and a man who had briefly dated her and nobody else. "I think this is it," Tony replied. "We can go ahead and get started."

He walked over to Mary. "Want me to carry Joey?"

"No, I've got him," she replied. Her gaze was soft and she offered him a sad smile. "Let's just say our final goodbyes to Amy."

Fifteen minutes later they all stood in a group just in front of the casket. It was rare that all of the cowboys were together and silence reigned, but everyone was quiet as they waited for Reverend Donaldson to speak. Tony had told the man as much as he could in an effort to give Amy a respectable eulogy.

"She was a child of God, but a troubled one," the reverend began. "She brought laughter and she brought tears to those around her…"

As Reverend Donaldson continued to speak, Tony

looked over to Mary and the child she held in her arms. Amy's boy. His boy. Memories of Amy exploded in his head. He'd met her at the Watering Hole on one of the rare nights when he'd gone with the other men to the bar.

She'd been a bright and shiny diamond on the dance floor and he'd been surprised when she'd grabbed him off a stool to dance with her.

They'd dated for two months before she'd moved to Oklahoma City and then they'd continued to see each other for two more months after that. She always drove to Bitterroot for their time together. He'd never seen where she was living in the city.

Now he knew she must have been living with Ash. With Amy's addiction and other issues she would have been drawn to a man like him. He would have been far more exciting than Tony.

When they'd split up, he hadn't given her another thought. She'd simply become a part of his past, and he'd never looked back.

No, he hadn't been in love with Amy, but he still grieved for her and for the sadness of her life and for the little boy she would never see grow to a man.

He focused back to the here and now and listened as Reverend Donaldson read several passages from the Bible. Tony glanced over to Mary, who had tears shining in her eyes as she looked at the casket. Halena had her eyes closed and her head bowed. They were both mourning the young girl they had known…the woman they had tried to save.

"Ashes to ashes, dust to dust…" Reverend Donald-son said.

Joey let out a loud mournful wail.

Tears blurred Tony's vision. It was as if the little boy mourned the fact that he no longer had a mother.

The sober mood of the funeral lifted as everyone gathered in the cowboy dining room for the noon meal. Cookie provided cold cuts for sandwiches, potato salad and chips and several salad options. There were huge chocolate chip cookies for dessert.

Mary was glad that Amy was finally at peace, but she ached for Joey. Amy had brought him to Tony out of love. She'd obviously known the danger she was in. She'd made the ultimate sacrifice in giving up her son to save his life. She hoped one day Joey would know that about his mother.

"Let me hold him and you go get something to eat," Tony said when they entered the dining room.

She relinquished the now happy baby to his father's arms and then she and Halena got into the food line. "Are you okay?" Halena asked her.

"I'm fine," she replied. "I'm glad this is over. We were so worried about her and now we don't have to worry any longer."

"Hopefully Ash Moreland will be arrested and then we definitely have no more worries," Halena replied. "Hmm, ambrosia salad. I love that stuff."

The two of them filled their plates and then went to the table where Tony sat with Joey. Cassie joined them along with Sawyer and Flint.

It wasn't long before life filled the room and removed the pall of the funeral. Sawyer held Joey while Tony went to get his plate of food.

They all filled their bellies and then several of the men moved the tables to the sides of the room and Mac got out his guitar.

"We said our goodbyes to Amy and now we celebrate life," Cassie said.

As if on cue, Mac started a rousing song that quickly had the men clapping their hands. "May I have this dance?" Clay asked Cassie.

The two of them began two-stepping across the floor. Everyone laughed as Jerod pulled up Flint and the two men hoofed it to the music.

Halena looked pointedly at Sawyer. He shot a frantic glance at Mary, who laughed as Halena grabbed him by the arm and yanked him onto the floor.

Tony grinned and patty-caked Joey's hands together in rhythm to the music while Mary's heart suddenly squeezed tight with a new impending grief. She was counting down the days to goodbye. The laughter and the fun and Tony holding Joey only made the coming goodbye that much more difficult.

At least you'll have memories. There would be many lonely nights ahead when all she would have were the memories of Joey's sweet snuggles against her and the wonder of his goofy, drooling grins.

At least you'll have memories. In the quiet before sleep she would remember Tony's scent, the way his smiles warmed her from head to toe. She would always have the memory of his body against hers and his kisses that torched a fire in her.

The memories would have to be enough. However, the picture of Tony laughing with Joey made her ache with the desire to belong to them.

"Mary, would you like to dance?" Adam asked.

"Sure." She got up from the bench, hoping that she could lose herself in the music instead of dwelling on the thoughts in her head.

The afternoon wore on and Mary danced with all of the cowboys, as did Cassie and Halena. When Mac took a break, Mary collapsed onto the bench next to Tony.

"I don't think I've ever danced this much in my entire life," she said half-breathlessly.

"You're a good partner. I saw that you easily maneuvered around Sawyer's three feet," he said in amusement.

She laughed. Sawyer might be handsome, but he definitely wasn't particularly graceful on the dance floor. "At least he didn't step on my toes."

"That's because you moved too fast."

"It doesn't look like Joey is going to move too fast too soon," she said as she gazed at the sleeping boy.

Tony patted him on the back. "It's a good thing he can sleep no matter what the noise level around him, but before the fun is over I'd like to have a dance with you."

Her heart stutter-stepped in her chest. "That would be fun," she said lightly. "Then I can say that I danced with every one of the Holiday cowboys."

He got his opportunity when Mac began playing again and Tony transferred Joey to Halena's lap. As he took Mary into his arms, she tried to still the frantic beat of her heart.

Even though the music was quick and lively, his hand was hot on her waist and his gaze was dark and hungry and the dance felt intimate and dangerous.

She was grateful when it ended and he released his hold on her. "I think I'm ready to call it a day," she said when they returned to the table.

It was after three when Jerod and Tony walked with the women back to the house. Halena and Cassie flew into the house with plans to make an elaborate evening meal despite the lunch they'd had.

Jerod was on house duty and decided to walk the perimeter of the house while Tony and Mary lingered just outside the back door.

Mary held Joey and smiled at Tony. "Amy would have been pleased that we all danced and had a good time today," she said.

He returned her smile. "Yeah, I think she would have liked the send-off," he agreed. He looked over toward the cemetery in the distance. "At least with her here I can take Joey to visit her occasionally when he gets old enough."

"You'll tell him that she loved him?" She stroked his downy dark hair.

"Absolutely. I'll tell him about her laughter and the sparkle in her eyes. I'll tell him all the good things and none of the bad."

Mary nodded. "Good."

"Mary, I don't care that you can't have children."

The words hung in the air.

"You already told me that," she replied stiffly.

"I just thought it might be a good time to remind you." There was a lightness in his voice, but the dark want in his eyes belied his tone.

"It's been a long day, Tony," she said wearily. "I'll see you tomorrow."

She turned and walked away from him, knowing that his gaze remained on her until she got inside the house and he could no longer see her.

Cassie and Halena were in the kitchen bustling around and Mary scooted through to the great room, where Joey's bouncy chair awaited him.

She placed him in the chair and then sank down on the sofa. She'd never felt as weary and as fragile as she did at this moment. Today had been a reminder that tomorrow wasn't promised. Anything could happen and suddenly your life would be over. If she died tomorrow, she'd take with her so many regrets, but they were regrets she couldn't fix.

The last thing she wanted was to walk away from Tony with a vision of revulsion on his face. She much preferred to walk away strong and proud with the memory of his love for her shining from his eyes.

"We ride tonight." The old garage smelled of gas and grease and stale cigarette smoke. The walls were spray-painted with obscene graffiti, but Ash didn't mind the surroundings. Before him were four of his most trusted men. They were mean, amoral men who would do anything Ash told them to do.

"It shouldn't be too hard to take out a couple of

dumb cowboys," Champ Waldron said as he squeezed an empty beer can and tossed it into a corner.

"I could use a little target practice." Jake the Snake sat on his lowrider and pointed his sawed-off shotgun around the room.

"Put that damned thing away," George snarled as he grabbed another beer from the cooler. "What time do you want this all to go down?"

"Let's meet back here at midnight," Ash replied. "It will be about an hour's drive to Bitterroot and at one in the morning all the men on the ranch should be sound asleep."

For the next half hour Ash explained his plans for the night and the layout of the Holiday ranch. When he was finished, the men left, but he knew they'd be back at midnight...the witching hour.

Ash grabbed himself a beer and sat on an old metal folding chair. He was too hot to stay in Oklahoma City when this was finished. Thankfully, he had plenty of money and several fake identifications to start a new life someplace else.

He'd been hearing reports that Florida had a big heroin problem. Sun and beach and a new business to grow, it definitely sounded like a plan.

And tonight he would get his son, the heir to Ash's business dealings. He cracked open the beer and took a long draw, then leaned back with a satisfied smile.

The men on the ranch would never know what hit them. He and his men would go in hard and fast. Ash would take what was his and then Ash Moreland and his son would disappear forever.

Chapter 15

Dinner consisted of beef Wellington, a cranberry salad, homemade rolls, a cream-cheese green-bean casserole and renewed heartache.

It was almost eight when the three women sat down to eat and Mary had been unable to get Tony out of her head no matter how hard she tried.

He doesn't care that I can't have children. Mary laughed as Halena said something outrageous. *We could adopt and fill a home with love.* The meal was utterly tasteless because Tony's words whirled around and around in her head.

But he would never be okay with her deformity. He'd run like Rick had and she just couldn't go through that kind of a trauma again. It was far better that he think she didn't love him. Eventually he'd get over her, but she had a feeling it would take a very long time for her to forget him.

"Granddaughter, food is meant to be eaten, not shoved around from place to place on your plate," Halena chided. "Cassie and I slaved over this glorious meal."

Mary flushed. "I'm sorry, I'm just not very hungry this evening. I ate so much at lunch. Besides, I saw the chocolate cake on the counter and you know that's my favorite. I don't want to get so full that I can't enjoy a huge piece of cake."

"And ice cream," Cassie added.

"And maybe a movie later?" Halena asked.

Cassie gave the old woman an affectionate grin. "And a movie later," she agreed.

Mary tried to stay focused through the rest of the meal and when she helped with the cleanup, but thoughts of Tony kept intruding.

After the cake and the ice cream had been eaten and they were all seated in the great room to watch the movie, the action on the big-screen television couldn't compete with the thoughts going around in Mary's head.

What kind of cruel fate had blown Tony into her life? How wicked was it to bring into her life a man she loved, a man she could never claim as her own?

It was time to say goodbye. Tony would care for Joey until he got them into an apartment or a house. She was no longer needed here.

She gazed down at Joey, who grinned back at her, and her heart wept knowing that she wouldn't see the baby again. She would no longer stand over his crib and watch him sleep. She wouldn't see his happy glee as he sucked on his bottle, or his delight when she carried on long conversations with him.

Tomorrow she and Halena would return to the house and get on with their ordinary lives and put all these extraordinary events behind them.

The boy and the man who had woven baskets of love in her heart would be forever banished, except perhaps in her deepest dreams.

It was almost eleven o'clock when she and Halena climbed the stairs for bed. The late meal and the movie had made it a long night. Mary put Joey down in his crib and then went into the room across the hall, where Halena had been sleeping.

The room held two twin beds and Halena sat on the foot of one of them with a red sparkly turban on her head. She reached up and touched it and preened. "A new gift from Cassie."

"Are you going to sleep in it?"

"I think if I wear it to bed I might dream-walk to a sparkly place."

"Tonight you dream-walk to someplace magical and tomorrow we go home."

Halena frowned. "The four of us?"

Mary shook her head. "No, just you and me."

Halena's frown deepened. "And so you won't give Tony Nakni a chance. He loves you, Mary."

Mary leaned against the doorjamb. "I know and knowing is enough for me."

"Tony is a much better man than Rick."

"But he's still a man," Mary protested. She drew in a deep breath and recognized since the moment Tony had entered her life she'd been wallowing in a self-pity that had been absent from her life for years.

Halena stood and walked over to her. She placed her hands on Mary's shoulders and peered at her intently. "You do yourself a disservice, my granddaughter, and I believe you do a disservice to Tony. You're strong and beautiful. You're a survivor."

"I am strong and I'm smart. I am a survivor and I have a wonderful, fulfilling life," she replied and straightened her shoulders. "I don't need a man to make me feel like a woman. For the last couple of weeks I've forgotten that I'm okay just the way I am."

"You're better than okay," Halena replied.

Mary nodded. "And tomorrow you and I go home alone and get on with our lives, and we won't speak of this again," she said firmly.

Halena dropped her arms back to her sides. "Then it is so," she replied. She walked back to the bed and sank down on the mattress. "But the leaves on the trees tell me you'll live with regret if you don't completely put your heart on the line with Tony."

"The leaves on the trees can whisper all they want, but my mind won't change," she retorted.

She returned to her own room, where she pulled on her nightgown and then crawled into bed. A new sense of peace drifted through her.

Certainly she would always ache for what would never be, but it was time to remember who she was—a strong, proud woman who had a good life.

Thankfully, she fell asleep immediately. She dreamed that she was standing on the edge of a cliff. A cold wind buffeted her and she knew the only way to get out of the icy wind was to jump. But she couldn't see what was beneath the cliff.

She was pulled from the dream and awakened by a loud clanging noise coming from someplace outside. She jumped out of bed and ran out of her room. She met Halena in the hallway.

"What's going on?" Mary asked as she flipped on the hallway light. "What's that bell?"

Halena shrugged and Cassie flew out of her bedroom, her eyes wide with fear. "It's the cowbell on the front porch," Cassie said. "It's only rung when there's an emergency."

At that moment the sound of motorcycles filled the air, followed quickly by gunfire.

Tony awakened to the ringing of the cowbell. He shot out of bed, his heartbeat thundering loudly in his ears. Jerod was on night guard duty and he'd ring the bell for only one reason.

Danger!

Above the cowbell, the roar of motorcycles broke the silence of the night. Then gunfire. What the hell? Tony pulled on his jeans and a T-shirt, then grabbed his gun and cracked open his door.

In the spill of moonlight, four motorcycles were visible. They raced around, tearing up the yard and shooting indiscriminately in all directions.

Ash.

The name boomed in Tony's head.

He was here for his son and he'd brought his army

to help him. Tony's blood froze as he gripped his gun firmly in his hand.

Doors began to creak open in the cowboy motel, letting Tony know the other men were awake. They would have their own guns and there was a potential for a bloodbath.

The night had gone mad. The men on the motorcycles were like marauding thugs from hell who were bent on destruction. It was impossible to see any of their faces. They were just dark silhouettes with headlights beaming brightly.

"What in the hell?" Sawyer stepped out of his room and into the open and then yelped and stumbled back into his room.

Tony's heart plummeted. Had Sawyer been shot? Was he hurt badly? Somehow Tony needed to get to him and check on his condition. Dammit, this was all his fault and the last thing he wanted was for any of the cowboys to get hurt.

He opened his door a little more and fell to the ground, hoping the darkness of the night would cover him enough for him to get to Sawyer's room.

Despite the coolness of the night his hands were sweaty and even above the roar of the motorcycles he heard his heartbeat pounding in his ears.

He crawled to Sawyer's door and only rose up enough to turn the doorknob and open the door. He threw himself into the room, slammed the door behind him and stood. Sawyer was on the bed, a bloody towel pressed to his shoulder.

"How bad is it?" Tony asked.

"I think it's just a flesh wound, but it's made me mad enough to hurt somebody," Sawyer replied.

Tony gazed at his friend worriedly. He didn't look like he was going to hurt anyone anytime soon. His face was pale and it was obvious he was in pain.

Gunfire still rang out and Tony worried what other casualties might happen before this night was over. "I've got to get to the house," he said urgently. "Are you sure you're okay?"

"I'm fine. Go," Sawyer replied.

Tony had to get to the women and Joey and make sure they were okay, make sure they stayed safe. That was where Ash would go, and he needed to make sure he got there before Ash did.

"Call Dillon," he said to Sawyer and then he opened the door and slid out into the chaos of the night.

He crouched just outside of Sawyer's room and watched the men on the motorcycles tearing back and forth, hooting and shooting. It was like a macabre scene from one of Halena's B-rated action flicks, except the danger was real and the bullets were deadly.

Adam crawled up next to him. "Tony, you okay?" He had to yell to be heard above the revving engines.

"Yeah, I'm okay. Sawyer took a bullet in the shoulder. I need to get to the house. I know Jerod was on guard duty tonight, but I don't know where he is now." The cowbell had stopped ringing minutes after the motorcycles had arrived and Tony worried about what might have happened to Jerod.

An urgent frustration filled him. All the lights in the house were on, like beacons crying out for help through the dark night. The house appeared a hundred miles away and there were crazed men on motorcycles with guns between him and the house where he needed to be. The air was thick with the acrid odors of gunpowder and gasoline.

"If I can get to the stables, from there I could probably make my way to the house," Tony said. Several shots rang out from the doorways of the bunkhouse.

Tony turned his head to look behind them and saw several shadows racing across the lawn with guns blazing. As a couple of the motorcycles veered off in their direction, Tony prayed none of his other "brothers" got hurt.

"I'll try to cover you," Adam replied. "On the count of three."

Tony drew in a deep breath, and when Adam got to three, he took off running. Adam fired a blaze of bullets as Tony raced across the open ground.

He got halfway to the stables before he caught one of the riders' attention. The motorcycle turned to give chase.

"Yahoo!" the driver yelled, and if Tony hadn't cut right and slid to the ground, the motorcycle would have struck him. As it was, it passed so close Tony felt the heat of the engine.

He got to his feet and ran, but a look over his shoulder let him know the motorcycle had turned around and was bearing down on him again.

As the driver began to fire his gun, Tony rolled to the ground, aimed and fired.

The driver cursed and lost control of his ride. Both

rider and motorcycle fell to the ground. The engine whined like a baby wanting a bottle as the man cursed and screamed.

Joey. Mary! He had to get to the house. Where were the women? Were they all huddled together in the great room? Upstairs in one of the bedrooms? And where was Ash Moreland?

With a burst of adrenaline, Tony managed to make it to the stables, where he ducked just inside the door. Where was Dillon? It felt as if hours had passed since he'd told Sawyer to call the law.

There was so much gunfire. His gut tightened and he swiped his sweaty gun hand on his jeans. People were going to be hurt. People were going to die tonight.

He peeked outside the door and cursed as he saw the two motorcycles zigzagging between him and the house. He had to get past them. He had a sinking, horrific terror that told him Mary and Joey were in immediate peril.

"Take Joey and go upstairs to your room," Cassie said urgently.

The three women had been standing helplessly in the great room while all hell broke loose outside. Cassie had been peering out the window since the commotion had begun and they had all come downstairs.

"Can you see Tony? Is he all right?" Mary asked as fear made her heart beat a million thumps a minute.

"It's too dark. I can't tell who is who, but the motorcycles are moving closer to the house. Please, Mary, go upstairs and hide in your room with the baby. You know he's who they're after."

Mary hugged Joey tightly against her chest. He'd been crying since the roar of the first motorcycle, as if he knew the danger he was in.

"Go, granddaughter," Halena said firmly.

Mary turned and hurried up the stairs. There was so much gunfire. Had Tony been hurt? Oh, God, was he lying out there bleeding? Had any of the other men been shot? Joey wailed as she turned into her bedroom.

She walked over to the side of the window and craned her neck to peer outside. She saw only dark silhouettes moving through the night and the headlights of the motorcycles as they roared back and forth across the yard.

She rocked Joey in her arms, trying to soothe him even as her fear rose so high she wanted to scream and cry with him. "It's all right, baby boy," she whispered. She tried to calm herself, hoping that would help him settle down.

He finally calmed down enough that she placed him in the crib and turned on the whirling mobile. He stared up at the dancing figures and waved his hands.

Protect him from evil and please protect Tony.

She turned around and gasped as the closet door flew open and Ash Moreland stepped out. "Little Mary Redbird," he said as he pointed his gun at her.

"My name is Mary Redwing," she replied, her voice nothing more than a trembling whisper. She leaned her back against the crib and stretched her arms out on either side of her to rest on the top of the railing.

Protect him from evil. The words once again screamed in her brain. Evil was now upon them.

"Whatever," he replied. "I appreciate you taking care of my boy, but now it's time he come home to Daddy."

"He's not your son, Ash. Amy was seeing another man and Joey is his son." Her entire body went cold as he narrowed his dark eyes. Frantically she glanced around for something she could use as a weapon, but there was nothing that could equal his gun.

"You're a liar," he snarled. "Now give him to me."

Mary tightened her grip on the railing. "I'd rather die than allow you to have him."

"That can be arranged. I'll give you to the count of three to move away from that crib so I can get my boy. One…"

Sirens sounded in the distance. "The police are coming. Just go," she exclaimed. "If you hurry, you can get out of here before they arrest you."

"I'm not leaving without my son. Two…"

Mary could only pray that the sound of his gunfire would bring somebody running and they would save Joey before Ash could escape with him.

There was no way she was going to step aside or hand Joey over to this monster. She sent up a silent prayer that Joey and Tony would survive this night and that Halena wouldn't mourn her too deeply.

"Three."

Tony flew through the door at the same time Ash fired his gun. The bullet intended for Mary slammed into his body at the same time he shot Ash.

Both Ash and Tony fell to the floor. Mary screamed

and Joey wailed. She ran to Tony, horrified to see a blossom of red on the front of his shirt.

"Tony?" Tears half blinded her as she fell to the floor at his side.

"Is he dead?" Tony's eyes were at half-mast and his breathing was labored. "Did I kill him?"

Mary glanced over to Ash. The bullet had caught him in his throat and there was no doubt that the man was dead. "Yes...yes, he's dead."

"Good." His eyes drifted closed.

"Stay with me, Tony," she cried.

His eyes fluttered open. "Mary, take good care of Joey," he gasped just before his eyes closed and didn't open again.

"Tony! Tony, open your eyes and talk to me," Mary screamed as tears blurred her vision. He'd taken the bullet meant for her and now he was dying.

A grief she'd never known before ripped through her. He'd sacrificed himself for her and for the son he loved.

"Mary... Mary, get up and let them attend to him." Halena's voice pierced through the sheer agony that gripped her. She looked up to see two EMTs. It was only then she realized the sound of the motorcycles had stopped.

"Help him," she said as she got up to her feet. "Hurry, he's been shot."

Cold. She was so cold. She wanted Tony's arms around her to warm her. She needed him to get up and tell her everything was going to be okay.

But he didn't awaken as they loaded him on a

stretcher. His utter stillness frightened her more than Ash's gun pointed at her chest.

Halena walked over to the crib and picked up Joey, who still cried. *Take good care of Joey.* Just before they were ready to carry Tony down the stairs she leaned down to him. "I will not take care of your son. You need to be strong. You need to be okay and take care of him yourself," she whispered.

He didn't move.

She followed them down the stairs, where police officers were in the kitchen with Cassie and several of the cowboys. "There's a dead man upstairs," she said to anyone who might listen. "I've got to get to the hospital."

"I'll take you," Juan Ramirez said.

"And I'll go upstairs." Officer Mike Jeffries pulled his gun and left the room.

The ambulance had already taken off by the time Mary got outside the back door. In a daze, she took in all the activity before her. Another ambulance was parked with Sawyer sitting in the back. A man clad in dirty jeans and a black leather jacket sat on the ground, cursing a blue streak as he pressed a towel to his upper arm.

Two men were in the back of Dillon's patrol car, and when Dillon saw her, he hurried over to where she stood. "Are you all right?"

"Tony got shot and he killed Ash. Ash is upstairs and he's dead," she said. Dillon gestured for two more men to go into the house.

"I told her I'd take her to the hospital," Juan said.

Dillon nodded. "Mary, I'll meet you there when I can. I've still got a mess to clean up here."

Minutes later she sat in the passenger seat of Juan's patrol car as they headed to the small hospital in town. The daze that had descended on her when she'd gone downstairs still had hold of her.

"At least it's over now," Juan said. "With Ash dead you don't have to be afraid anymore."

"Yes, it's over." She stared out the passenger window. It was over, but at what cost? Tony might die. He might already be dead.

The thought caused the air to whoosh from her lungs and blew a bleak coldness through her entire body. He had to be alive. He just had to be okay. Joey needed him now more than ever.

Juan pulled into the hospital emergency room parking lot and together they got out of the car. Mary ran ahead of him and entered the empty waiting room. A receptionist sat behind a glass window.

"Can I help you?" she asked after opening the window.

"Tony Nakni, I need to know how he's doing." Mary was vaguely aware of Juan standing just behind her. "He was just brought in by ambulance."

"I'll go check. I'll be right back." She slammed the window closed and disappeared.

Mary continued to stare at the window, willing the woman to come back and tell her that Tony was just fine and he would walk out of the emergency room doors at any moment.

Every nerve in her body tensed as seconds ticked by.

"He's tough, Mary," Juan said softly.

"Nobody is tough when a bullet flies," she replied.

Finally the woman returned to the window. "He's in surgery now. The doctor told me to tell you to prepare for a long wait."

A long wait? That could only mean he was badly hurt. Mary's knees buckled and Juan took her by the elbow and guided her to one of the chairs.

She collapsed and prepared herself for an endless night.

Chapter 16

Full consciousness came to Tony slowly. His first awareness was the click and whir of some sort of a machine, then the unmistakable antiseptic smell of a hospital.

His mind was a bit fuzzy. The last thing he remembered was Ash's deep voice counting down to shoot Mary and grab Joey.

What had happened? He'd shot at Ash. Had he hit him? Or had he missed and fallen unconscious, leaving the two people he loved more than anything on the face of the earth in danger?

He snapped open his eyes and tried to sit up but released a small groan as pain shot through his lower chest on the left side.

It was then he saw her.

Mary.

She was slumped back in the chair by the window, her head turned to face him as she slept. He breathed a sigh of relief. She wouldn't be sleeping in his hospital room if any danger remained.

Despite the dark shadows that clung beneath her eyes, in spite of the tousled strands of her hair, she was the most beautiful thing he'd ever seen.

He'd been looking at her for about ten minutes when her eyes slowly opened. "Tony!" She jumped out of the chair and came to the side of his bed. "How do you feel?" A worry furrow appeared across her forehead.

"A little confused and sore. How long have I been here?" He could smell her now, that glorious scent of mysterious spices, that fragrance that seeped into his blood and wrapped around his heart.

"Two days. The bullet broke one of your ribs and the doctor did laparoscopy surgery to check things out."

"And how are things?"

She smiled. "You were lucky. The bullet didn't do any other damage. You're going to be good as new in a couple of weeks. Now that you're awake I'm sure the doctor will let you go home in the next day or so to recuperate."

"Where's Joey?"

"With Cassie and Grandmother. I—I needed to be here with you." Tears misted her beautiful eyes. "You took a bullet for me, Tony. You could have been killed."

"I'd gladly take a bullet for you anytime. What about Ash?"

"He's dead and two of his men were shot and two

more were arrested. He won't bother us anymore, Tony. The danger is finally over."

Tony couldn't work up a single ounce of guilt over the man he had killed. "And the rest of the men at the ranch?" he asked worriedly.

"Sawyer suffered a flesh wound to the shoulder and Jerod has a concussion. Ash knocked him over the head to get into the house by the front door. Thank God everyone else is okay."

Thank God. The last thing he wanted was to be responsible for any of the men getting hurt or killed. They had all put their lives on the line by leaving their rooms and confronting his danger head-on.

"Have you been here for the last two days?" he asked.

"I couldn't leave until I knew you were really going to be okay."

He searched her features. A woman who didn't love him wouldn't stay in his hospital room for two long days. A woman who didn't love him wouldn't be looking at him now with tears in her eyes.

"Mary…"

He only got her name out before she stepped back, her eyes dark and guarded. "I've made arrangements with Clay to take us home. Cassie has said she'll watch Joey as long as you need her to. I was just waiting for you to wake up so I could tell you goodbye."

Goodbye. The word hung heavy between them. He didn't understand her choice. He would go to his grave believing that Mary Redwing loved him. But he wasn't going to fight for her anymore.

"Mary, I'll never be able to thank you for what you've

done for me. I promised you a paycheck for watching Joey and as soon as I get out of this bed I'll see to it."

"Don't worry about it. Having you...having Joey in my life for a little while is payment enough." She took another step backward and the mist in her eyes grew thicker. "Be well, Tony, and live a happy life."

She spun out of the room as if the very devil himself was on her tail. He squeezed his eyes tightly closed. The pain that ripped through him was far worse than any physical injuries he might have suffered.

She was gone and there was nothing he could do about it. By the time he got out of the hospital there would be no trace of her left at the ranch.

It was time for him to move on. He had a life to build with a little boy who needed him. He turned his head toward the window and stared out. The danger was truly over and it was a beautiful day. He'd loved...and he'd lost, but he was alive and he was a strong, proud man who would survive.

"I hear my patient is awake."

Tony turned his head to see Dr. Wendall Johnson entering the room. "I'm awake," Tony replied, although he'd rather be in a deep sleep of oblivion right now. "When can I get out of here?"

He had a house to rent and a life to build with the little boy who was now an orphan unless the DNA results came back and proved he was Joey's father. And if the results came back that he was not Joey's father, then he would find the appropriate authorities and begin the adoption process.

Hopefully, the fact that he was a single man wouldn't

hurt his chances of adopting Joey. No matter what it took, he'd do it in order to keep the little boy in his life.

With the doctor's promise that if all went well he could be released the next day, Tony took a nap. When he awakened, he was surprised to see Halena seated in the chair where Mary had been earlier in the day. Twilight was falling outside the window and Halena had on her lucky casino blouse.

"Aren't you supposed to be playing slot machines?" he asked.

"That's where Mary thinks I am."

"So what are you doing here?"

"Can't I come to visit a friend?"

"Of course," Tony replied. He struggled to sit up. "You're doing okay?"

"I'm sore, but I'm doing well enough that the doctor said I might get to go home tomorrow."

"That's good. I've grown very fond of you, Tony Nakni." She leaned forward, her gaze intent. "And the leaves on the trees tell me you love my granddaughter very much."

Tony released a small, slightly bitter laugh. "You don't need the trees on the leaves to tell you. I'm more than happy to tell you I love Mary with all my heart."

"As she does you." Halena sat back in the chair. Tony stared at her in frustration. "How hard are you willing to fight for her? How much do you love her? A good warrior fights for what he wants."

"I have fought for her," he replied. "And she keeps telling me she doesn't love me."

"She's afraid."

"Afraid of what?"

"It's not my place to say, but if you want to win her heart, then you have to force her to tell you her secret." Halena rose. "And now Mabel is waiting for me and those slot machines are calling."

"Halena," he protested. "What secret? Tell me."

"Fight for her, Tony," she said as she flew out the door.

He half rose and shouted her name, but she was gone. He slumped back in the bed, more confused than ever. What kind of a secret could Mary possibly have that was keeping her from love?

Mary sat in her new, bigger and better back porch and watched the raindrops sliding down the windows. The rain had begun just after noon and still continued as day transformed into night.

Tony would be out of the hospital by now. He and little Joey would be in his bunk room at the ranch. Or perhaps Cassie had invited him to stay in the big house, in the bedroom where she and Joey had stayed until he could get settled in someplace else.

She frowned and focused on the blouse she'd been beading. She was waiting on a delivery of river cane from her distributor in Louisiana before she could begin working on baskets again.

Why was she thinking about Tony and Joey? They were so yesterday's news. It had been well over twenty-four hours ago when she'd told him goodbye.

And the rain kept falling down.

She'd hoped that she and her grandmother might

enjoy a movie night tonight, but Halena had gone to the casino again with Mabel. Who knew what time her grandmother would finally roll in?

Mary supposed she could watch a movie by herself. It might help take her mind off the pain that arrowed through her heart. Still, she couldn't work up enough enthusiasm about the plan to leave the porch.

She'd been stunned when she'd seen the back porch for the first time. The men Tony hired had made it so much bigger, and with the windows she could now work out here even on the rainiest day. He'd had vertical blinds hung that could be pulled to block out the sun if it got too warm, and a new worktable put in place. He'd even bought a big roomy wicker chair with a bright floral cushion that she knew was meant for Halena.

He'd thought of everything…because he loved her.

She got up from her chair. Maybe she'd put a movie on after all. She didn't want to sit and watch it rain anymore. She didn't want to think of Tony and Joey and loss any longer.

She'd just walked into the living room when a knock sounded at the door. Who, other than Halena, would be out on such a miserable night like this?

Tony.

Her stomach clenched. She'd already told him goodbye. Surely it couldn't be him. Maybe it was a neighbor needing something. Surely it couldn't be Tony.

She opened the door and there he stood, raindrops pattering on his shoulders and clinging to his dark, long lashes. "Mary, can I come in? I need to speak with you."

No. She didn't want to see him. She didn't want to

talk to him. She was over him. "Okay," she heard herself say. She couldn't very well keep him standing on the front porch in the rain, she told herself.

She stepped aside and he swept past her, his familiar scent fluttering a new sense of grief through her. Once they were in the living room, he shrugged off his coat and cast it aside, then turned to face her.

"Is Joey all right?" she asked.

"He's fine, but he misses you."

She steeled her heart, refusing to be moved by either the thought that the little boy might miss her, or the longing that filled Tony's eyes.

"Why are you here? We already said our goodbyes." She crossed her arms, as if to create a barrier against him and against the aching love he evoked in her.

"I'm here for answers." His dark eyes bore into hers. "I know you love me, Mary. Even your grandmother knows what's in your heart for me. So, I'm here and I don't intend to leave until you tell me the secret that is keeping you from me."

"Secret?" Her blood chilled. "I don't know what you're talking about."

He took several steps toward her. "Halena seemed to know and she thought it was important that you tell me."

"She's a meddling fool," she replied. *Oh, Grandmother, why didn't you keep your nose out of this?*

"I think she's a very wise woman. She knows how much I love you and she knows how much you love me." He took another step forward, standing far too close to her now. "Tell me, Mary. Tell me your secret, make me understand why you aren't in my arms right now."

She stared at him. She suddenly remembered the dream she'd had of standing on a cliff as a frigid wind buffeted her. She was about to jump into the dark abyss.

She hadn't wanted him to know. She hadn't wanted to see him turn away from her. But Halena had forced her hand by saying too much to him.

"You want to know my secret? Fine," she snapped. "Follow me."

She led him into the privacy of her bedroom and then turned to look at him. This was the moment she'd hoped would never happen. But she had a feeling Tony might never go away unless he saw her secret. That would certainly make him hightail it out of her life.

And it would make her hate him just a little bit.

"Mary?" He looked at her curiously.

"When I got ovarian cancer, because my mother and one of my aunts had died of breast cancer, the doctor did genetic testing on me. I found out I had the BRCA gene mutation."

He frowned. "I'm sorry, I don't know what that means."

"It meant I had a good chance of getting breast cancer and possibly dying like my mother. So, I took them off." A small burst of slightly hysterical laughter escaped her. "I said off with their heads."

The laughter turned into an unexpected sob. "I don't have real breasts, Tony. All I have is this." With a deep breath she grabbed the bottom of her T-shirt and tore it off over her head.

She stood before him defiantly, steeling herself for his reaction.

He stared at her for several long moments. "Mary,

Mary." He shook his head and took a couple of steps toward her. "Did you really believe that I fell in love with your breasts? Did you really think that this would somehow change my feelings for you?"

A trembling began at the center of her as she searched his features, looking for the revulsion she was so certain she would see. All she saw was the sweet gaze of a man who loved her.

He took another step and then covered her breasts with his hands. He ran his fingers over the scars, his gaze holding hers intently.

"Tony." His name slid from her lips on a sigh of wonder.

"You are so beautiful."

"I don't have much of any feeling there," she said, still stunned by his reaction.

"If you can't feel me touching you here, then feel me touching you in your heart." He leaned down and kissed across each scar.

She didn't feel the sweetness of his mouth on her breasts, but her heart did feel his kisses, heating with the flames of the love that she'd tried to deny.

"Are you real?" she asked breathlessly. "Is this real?"

He raised his head and gazed at her with eyes that spoke of forever. "This is very real. I'm so glad you made the choice you did so that we could be together now and build a future. I want you, Mary. I want you today and every day for the rest of my life."

His mouth covered hers in a fiery kiss that banished all her doubts, all her fears. He loved her and he thought she was beautiful.

For the first time in years she felt beautiful, scars and all, and what she wanted more than anything at this moment was to lie naked in his arms. She wanted his passion for her…and hers for him to explode.

"Make love to me, Tony."

"With pleasure," he replied.

He stepped away from her only long enough for the two of them to completely undress, then they fell into her bed and she was in his arms, her naked breasts against the warmth of his chest as he kissed her long and hard.

"Marry me, Mary," he said when the kiss ended. "Tell me you'll marry me."

A wild exhilaration filled her. "I'll marry you," she replied.

He kissed her again and then their hands moved to explore each other with the slowness of discovery that had been lacking the last time they'd made love.

Everything was intensified by the knowledge that her secret was out—he'd seen her scars and he still wanted her, he still loved her.

His hands slid languidly down the length of her, each touch shooting shimmering fireworks through her and at the same time she tangled her hands in his long hair, moved to caress the width of his back and grabbed his firm buttocks.

He was fully aroused but seemed to be in no hurry. She gasped as his fingers danced along her inner thigh and then touched the very core of her.

"Tony." His name whispered out of her as every nerve in her body electrified.

"You're in my blood, Mary. I'll never stop loving you," he said just before he took her mouth with his once again.

As the kiss went on, his fingers moved faster against her and her heartbeat raced faster as she climbed to a precipice of tension that finally exploded in her veins.

She cried out with the release and he moved between her thighs and entered her. Their gazes locked as he moved inside her, slowly bringing her alive once again.

Their gasping breaths filled the room as she thrust her hips to meet his. Faster and faster…harder and harder they moved until tears of joy filled her eyes and she shuddered with another climax.

He stiffened with his own release and then collapsed next to her. For several long minutes they didn't speak, they only stared into each other's eyes and spoke of love without needing the words.

He finally released a deep sigh and reached up and slid a finger down her cheek. "We belong together, Mary. You and me and Joey, we're all going to be a family."

"I want that, Tony. I want it more than you'll ever know." She frowned. "But you know I'm a package deal. I would never leave my grandmother."

"How about you don't go anywhere and you just make room for me and Joey right here."

"That would be okay with you?"

He laughed. "Mary, I would live in a tent if that's what you wanted to do. Besides, I wouldn't want to miss one of Halena's hat days or not know what the leaves on the trees were whispering to her."

Mary laughed and cuddled against him, her heart more full than it had ever been in her life. "Now tell me what our life together is going to look like."

"I'll move in here and I'd still like to work on the Holiday ranch if that's okay with you. I'll be home in the evenings and on my days off to help you with chores and taking care of the children."

She raised her head to look at him once again. "Children?"

"We should probably see about adopting a sister for Joey to start."

"To start?"

He returned her grin. "Who knows how many children we might end up with."

"And this from a man who professed he didn't want children," she teased.

"That was before I knew love. We're going to have a wonderful life together, Mary."

She believed him. She leaned over and kissed him, a kiss that held all her love, all her hopes and dreams. He was the man she'd been waiting for, a man who would love her despite her flaws.

He made her feel beautiful and free. She was a survivor and for the first time a true sense of pride swept through her. She had made difficult life choices to be here now, to live life to the fullest with the man who held her heart.

Epilogue

Tony sat on the sofa next to Mary and little Joey was on a blanket on the floor, chattering and kicking his legs as if he knew the next few minutes were very important to him.

Halena sat in the chair facing them, clad in zebra-striped sleep pants and a bright-colored floral house dress. Perched on the top of her head was the sequined red turban Cassie had given her.

The envelope containing the DNA results was in the middle of the coffee table just waiting to be opened.

He and Joey had become permanent residents in the house a week ago and it had been the best week in Tony's life. Gone were the ghosts of his past, vanished was the bitterness that had once filled his soul.

Mary's love had healed him, as he hoped his love

had done the same for her. He would go through his miserable childhood all over again if it meant that he would now be here with her. She still took his breath away with a simple smile.

"Is anyone going to open that or are we going to sit around and stare at it all evening?" Halena asked. She reached up and straightened the turban on her braided hair.

Tony leaned forward and picked up the envelope. "You know it doesn't matter to me what the test shows." He looked down at Joey, who laughed and drooled down his chin. Tony's heart expanded in his chest. "I love Joey no matter what. I intend to be his father for the rest of his life." Still, there was no question that things would be easier if the test revealed that Joey was Tony's biological son.

Mary leaned over and took his hand in hers. "No matter what happens we'll fight for him." She gave his hand a squeeze and then released it.

Yes, they would jump through whatever bureaucratic hoops they needed to in order to keep Joey in their lives. They would deal with any red tape that might come with legally adopting him.

He was surprised that his fingers trembled as he tore open the envelope. Nervous tension welled up inside him. He wanted this. He wanted this so badly.

For just a moment memories of Amy rushed through his head. When Joey got old enough, Tony would tell him about his mother, about the good qualities she'd possessed.

But Mary would be the mother who would bake cookies and tuck him in at night. She would provide the soft touches, the unconditional love of a true mother.

And Halena? She would be the grandmother who all his friends envied, the one who would tell him stories and make him laugh and probably embarrass him on more than one occasion.

"I'm getting older by the minute," Halena said impatiently.

Tony pulled out the sheet of paper that would answer the question. Was it him…or was it Ash?

He read the paper—99.998. That was the percentage that declared Tony to be Joey's biological father. Rich emotion pressed so tightly in his chest he couldn't speak.

"Well?" Halena leaned forward.

"It's me," he gasped. "Thank God, it's me." He laughed with sheer exhilaration and jumped up from the sofa. He reached down and picked up Joey in his arms and began to dance around the room.

"I'm your daddy, Joey." He reached out and grabbed Mary's hand and pulled her up. "And this is your mama and we're going to have a wonderful life together."

He grabbed Mary around her waist and pulled her close enough to kiss her. When the kiss ended, her eyes shone with promise and love and his heart had never been so full.

"I'll be right back. I have a little surprise," Halena said.

"Should we be afraid?" Tony asked when Halena disappeared down the hallway.

"Maybe a little," Mary replied with a grin. She pulled a tissue from her pocket and wiped Joey's drool from his chin.

"It's definitely a hat kind of a day," Halena said as she returned to the room. Now she wore a yellow hat that resembled a large bird's nest and she had her hands behind her back.

"You aren't going to make me wear a hat, are you?" Tony asked suspiciously.

"Of course not. I wouldn't want to detract from your natural handsomeness," she replied with a grin. She walked over to where Tony stood with Joey in his arms.

"Joey, I'm your grandmother and it's my job to teach you to love Mexican food and listen to the leaves on the trees and know when it's a good day for a hat."

She pulled out a tiny brown felt cowboy hat that closely resembled Tony's cowboy hat and she put it on Joey's head. "And now you are truly your father's son. And that's that."

Joey laughed and tilted his head as if showing off his new hat. And then they were all laughing and hugging and Tony knew he was finally home. He had a woman he loved with all his heart, another woman who would keep them all on their toes and the little boy who had turned him into a father.

Yes, he was finally home and he had a feeling big Cass and Amy were together and smiling down on them all from Heaven.

He gazed at Mary and Halena and then back at his son. This was his circle of love.

* * *

Dillon finished reading over the final report of the action that had occurred at the Holiday ranch and then leaned back in his chair and sighed.

It had been damned lucky that more people hadn't died that night. Thankfully Tony had survived and Sawyer had suffered only a minor wound to the shoulder. Things could have been so much worse.

Of course, Ash was dead and two of his men had been hospitalized. Once the two were well enough, they'd be transported from the hospital to jail to await sentencing on charges serious enough they wouldn't be bothering anyone else for a very long time.

Dillon had interviewed Mary and Tony in his investigation into Ash's death, but no charges would be brought against Tony. He'd acted in self-defense and Dillon was glad Ash Moreland was dead.

Since the tornado that had taken Cass's life and the arrival of Cassie Peterson in town, the universe had been in chaos. Dillon had been embroiled in more crimes in the past five months than he had been in the last five years.

He'd had to contend with a crazed ex-husband threatening Cassie's best friend, a murderous assistant attempting to kill the forensic anthropologist who had come to deal with the skeletal remains of the murdered young men and a deadly stalker who had nearly killed Trisha Cahill.

And that didn't account for the usual crimes that occasionally occurred in a small town. He was exhausted, but pleased that Tony and Mary no longer had to worry about somebody coming after them.

Hopefully things would go back to normal around town and he would get a breather. He closed his eyes and for a moment a sense of peace wafted through him.

It lasted only a moment as the tormented cries of seven unsolved murder victims screeched in his head.

* * * * *

If you loved this novel, don't miss other suspenseful titles by New York Times *bestselling author Carla Cassidy:*

COWBOY AT ARMS
COWBOY UNDER FIRE
COWBOY OF INTEREST
A REAL COWBOY

Available now from Harlequin Romantic Suspense!

REQUEST YOUR FREE BOOKS!
2 FREE NOVELS PLUS 2 FREE GIFTS!

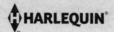

ROMANTIC suspense

Sparked by danger, fueled by passion

YES! Please send me 2 FREE Harlequin® Romantic Suspense novels and my 2 FREE gifts (gifts are worth about $10). After receiving them, if I don't wish to receive any more books, I can return the shipping statement marked "cancel." If I don't cancel, I will receive 4 brand-new novels every month and be billed just $4.74 per book in the U.S. or $5.49 per book in Canada. That's a savings of at least 12% off the cover price! It's quite a bargain! Shipping and handling is just 50¢ per book in the U.S. and 75¢ per book in Canada.* I understand that accepting the 2 free books and gifts places me under no obligation to buy anything. I can always return a shipment and cancel at any time. Even if I never buy another book, the two free books and gifts are mine to keep forever.

240/340 HDN GH3P

Name _____ (PLEASE PRINT) _____

Address _____ Apt. # _____

City _____ State/Prov. _____ Zip/Postal Code _____

Signature (if under 18, a parent or guardian must sign)

Mail to the **Reader Service:**
IN U.S.A.: P.O. Box 1867, Buffalo, NY 14240-1867
IN CANADA: P.O. Box 609, Fort Erie, Ontario L2A 5X3

Want to try two free books from another line?
Call 1-800-873-8635 or visit www.ReaderService.com.

* Terms and prices subject to change without notice. Prices do not include applicable taxes. Sales tax applicable in N.Y. Canadian residents will be charged applicable taxes. Offer not valid in Quebec. This offer is limited to one order per household. Not valid for current subscribers to Harlequin Romantic Suspense books. All orders subject to credit approval. Credit or debit balances in a customer's account(s) may be offset by any other outstanding balance owed by or to the customer. Please allow 4 to 6 weeks for delivery. Offer available while quantities last.

Your Privacy—The Reader Service is committed to protecting your privacy. Our Privacy Policy is available online at www.ReaderService.com or upon request from the Reader Service.

We make a portion of our mailing list available to reputable third parties that offer products we believe may interest you. If you prefer that we not exchange your name with third parties, or if you wish to clarify or modify your communication preferences, please visit us at www.ReaderService.com/consumerschoice or write to us at Reader Service Preference Service, P.O. Box 9062, Buffalo, NY 14240-9062. Include your complete name and address.

HRS15

*When Piper Colton is accused of murdering her
adoptive father, she sets out to prove her innocence with
a little help from PI Cord Maxwell. Too bad her brother
hired him first—to bring her in for skipping bail...*

*Read on for a sneak preview of
RUNAWAY COLTON,
the penultimate book in
THE COLTONS OF TEXAS miniseries.*

Whatever Piper's intention, her words coaxed a reluctant
smile from him. "It's the truth," Cord insisted, merely
because he wanted to see what she'd do next. "I never lie."

"Never?"

"Never."

She circled him, keeping several feet between them.

"That must make life difficult for you sometimes."

Thoroughly entertained, he acknowledged her comment
with a nod.

"Do you like me?" No coquettishness in either her
voice or her expression, just simple curiosity.

"Yes. Actually, I'm beginning to," he amended, still
smiling. "Why do you want to know?"

She shrugged. "Just testing to see if you really won't
lie. Are you attracted to me?"

A jolt went through him. "Are you flirting?"

Though she colored, she didn't look away. "Maybe.
Maybe not. I'm trying to find out where we stand with
each other. I also noticed you didn't answer the question."

He laughed; he couldn't help it. "I'd have to be dead not to find you attractive," he told her. "But don't worry, I won't let it get in the way of the job I have to do. Or finding Renee. Both are too important to me."

Color still high, she finally smiled back. "Fair enough. Now how about we call it a night and regroup in the morning."

Though it was still early, he nodded. "Okay. Good night."

She sighed. "I'm probably going to regret this, but…"

Before he could ask what she meant, she crossed the space between them, grabbed him and pulled him down for a kiss. Her mouth moved across his, nothing tentative about it. A wave of lust swamped him. Damn if it wasn't the most erotic kiss he'd ever shared.

Standing stock-still, he let her nibble and explore, until he couldn't take it any longer. Finally, he seized control, needing to claim her. He tasted her, skimmed his fingers over her soft, soft skin, outlining her lush curves. He couldn't get enough, craving more, breathing her in until the force of his arousal told him he needed to break it off right now or they'd be in trouble.

He'd be in trouble, he amended silently. Despite the fact that he physically shook with desire, he stepped back, trying to slow his heartbeat and the way he inhaled short gasps of air. Drowning—that's what this had been like. Drowning in her.

Don't miss
RUNAWAY COLTON by Karen Whiddon,
available November 2016 wherever
Harlequin® Romantic Suspense
books and ebooks are sold.

www.Harlequin.com

HRSEXP1016

JUST CAN'T GET ENOUGH?

Join our social communities
and talk to us online.

You will have access to the latest
news on upcoming titles and special
promotions, but most importantly,
you can talk to other fans about your
favorite Harlequin reads.

Harlequin.com/Community

Facebook.com/HarlequinBooks

Twitter.com/HarlequinBooks

Pinterest.com/HarlequinBooks